The Noble Widow

Book 1 of the Lodero Westerns

Robert Peecher

For information the author may be contacted at

PO Box 967; Watkinsville GA; 30677

or at robertpeecher.com

This is a work of fiction. Any similarities to actual events in whole or in part are purely accidental. None of the characters or events depicted in this novel are intended to represent actual people.

CONTENTS

1

The three riders in black coats and hats drew the usual notice of strangers coming into town. That is to say, they drew considerable notice. This wasn't the sort of village where strangers often turned up, and already another stranger had rode into town earlier in the day.

Marshal Walt Sanders, sitting by the window inside the Dry Gulch Saloon, sipped from a cup of coffee and stirred his corned beef and cabbage with his fork. As marshal, it was Walt's job to be suspicious when strangers rode to town, but these three men brought suspicion on themselves. They carried themselves like ruffians. Their posture, the scowls on their faces, the six-shooters on their hips -- everything about them seemed constructed to intimidate.

The thick dust and inescapable heat conspired to clog the throat and drain a man of all his desire to get up and do anything, so the street was pretty empty so long as the afternoon sun was beating down on it. The cowpunchers who would be drinking in the saloon later were all still working on their ranches, so there was no liveliness in the town. No womenfolk were shopping and no menfolk were doing business. When the three riders pulled reins in front of the Dry Gulch Saloon, swung out of their saddles, and hitched their horses, they were the only men on the street. They stood on the boardwalk out front of the Dry Gulch for a minute, talking among themselves and looking over the town. Marshal Sanders wondered if he should send someone for Joe Dixon, his deputy. These men looked like they were going to be trouble.

Walt looked around the Dry Gulch to see where he might find support if things went poorly.

Dale Burton behind the bar would be no use. Dale had a shotgun behind the bar, but he would never use it.

Connie Wade was sitting at the bar, but he was too drunk to shoot straight and didn't carry a gun anyway.

The rancher Wayne McClellan and two of his cowpunchers were each having a beer. Wayne and his two men all carried a gun on their hips, and they might throw those guns if these three riders brought trouble inside the saloon. Wayne was the type of man who would back up the marshal if he needed it.

There was also the stranger in the back, bent over his plate of food and eating like he'd not eaten in a week. His whiskey sat on the table untouched -- he paid for the whiskey just to get the free lunch. When Walt first came into the Dry Gulch and saw the stranger sitting in the back of the saloon, he asked Dale about him.

"Says he come to town looking for work," Burton had said. "Says he's good with hawses."

"Has he talked to anyone about a job?" Walt had

2

asked.

"Not yet. He got a whiskey and went to the buffet and now he's eatin'. That's as long as he's been here."

At the time, Walt didn't give the stranger another thought. But now he wondered if this stranger had anything to do with the arrival of the three men out front.

Walt watched him for a moment. The stranger looked up at the open doorway of the saloon, looking at the men who'd just ridden up. He shoveled a couple of last bites of food into his mouth and then turned up his whiskey into his mouth. This was a man who was finishing in a hurry. Marshal Walt Sanders reached down and thumbed the leather loop off the hammer of his gun. He had a feeling he'd be drawing it shortly.

The stranger stood up, his back to the back wall of the saloon, and he did not move from that spot. He was wearing a tan colored, light-weight duster over a black vest and black-and-white checkered shirt. He wore a broad brimmed, flat-crowned black hat. As the stranger pulled the duster back away from his thighs, Walt saw that the man wore a six-shooter on each hip. Spurs and the heavy footfalls of boots on boards alerted Marshal Sanders that the three men outside were now walking into the Dry Gulch, and he turned his attention back to the front of the saloon.

The men took several steps inside. Their eyes took a few moments to adjust from the bright sun outside to the dim light inside, and they did not move farther into the saloon until they could see clearer. All three of them looked at Walt Sanders, but their menacing gazes moved on. At first sight, they had no respect for Walt Sanders or the star on his chest. Marshal Sanders watched them as their eyes lit on the stranger at the back of the saloon. They'd not seen him initially -- motionless the way he was, the stranger had a way of blending into the shadows. Especially for men coming into a dark room from blazing sunlight outside, the stranger at the back was not easy to see, and Walt wondered if he'd planned it that way.

What worried Marshal Walt Sanders was the way the three men appeared startled when they saw the stranger in the back. Three men who ride into town with the obvious design of intimidation shouldn't scare easy, but these men sure seemed to. Sanders wondered if their reactions spoke more about the three men, or more about the stranger in the back of the saloon.

"What'll you have boys?" Dale Burton called from behind the bar, and Walt Sanders was dumbfounded at how oblivious Dale could be sometimes.

Walt dropped his hand down to the grip of his revolver, but he did not yet stand up.

The three men stood shoulder to shoulder. One of them answered the saloon keeper. "We ain't here for you, old man, and be glad of it."

"We come for you Lodero," the man in the center said. He was looking at the stranger at the back.

Wayne McClellan and his two cowpunchers, who'd read the tension the moment the three strangers walked in, slid back their chairs and moved over toward the bar so that they wouldn't be in the center of the room when the shooting started. Marshal Sanders made a mental note to remember that he couldn't count on Wayne McClellan to back him up.

"Now hold your horses," Walt Sanders said,

4

standing up. He kept his right hand on the grip of his gun as he stood, but he held out his left hand in front of him, trying to calm the men who'd just walked into the Dry Gulch in the same way he might hold out his hand to try to calm a frightened bronc. "I'm Marshal Walt Sanders. You boys want to tell me what's going on here?"

"We come for Lodero," the center man said, not looking at the marshal, not taking his eyes off the stranger in the back.

"I suppose you're Lodero?" Sanders asked the stranger.

"Folks call me that," the stranger said.

"And what do you boys want with him?" Walt Sanders asked.

"This ain't none of your concern, marshal," the man closest to Walt said. He turned, took his eyes off the stranger in the back, and looked right at Marshal Sanders. The man might have been startled when he saw Lodero in the back, but he had no fear of Walt Sanders.

"Sure it is my concern," Walt said. "You ride into my town, you walk in here looking like you're ready to shoot up the place. Of course it's my concern. So you boys calm down, and why don't you try telling me what's going on here."

The man closest to him took a step closer. Marshal Sanders, whose job required him to make quick judgments of men, immediately disliked this man. He had about him a cavalier attitude and showed a disrespect for the law. Walt knew, too, that he his quick judgments on a man's character were seldom wrong.

"It's like this, marshal. We're the posse, and we're

here to take Lodero back with us. It ain't your concern, and you'd be wise to stay out of it."

"Posse?" Walt asked. "What posse? From where?"

"We're the posse looking for Lodero for shooting a man back at Fort Concho. We intend to take him back there so that he can hang for what he done."

Marshal Sanders looked at the stranger with his back to the wall. The man had not moved. His eyes were locked on the three men at the front of the saloon.

Now the man in the center spoke, though he kept his eyes on the stranger in the back of the room.

"He shot my brother, marshal. You'd be wise to stay out of this."

"If you're a posse, let me see the warrant for this man," Sanders said.

Everything about these three men suggested to Walt Sanders that if they didn't shoot the stranger here in the Dry Gulch, they'd get him a little ways outside of town and hang him or shoot him there. He did not believe these men intended to take anyone to a trial anywhere. "I ain't inclined to let you take him without seeing a warrant."

The man facing Marshal Walt Sanders was the first to draw, but Walt didn't even realize what was happening before he heard the first gunshot.

The report of the gun was deafening inside the small saloon, and the ringing in Walt's ears disoriented him. But he realized that the gunshot had come from the stranger in the back of the saloon.

The man facing Walt dropped his gun and stumbled into the wall. That's when the marshal realized that the man facing him had been drawing a gun to shoot him. These three strangers rode into town, came into the Dry Gulch to interrupt his supper, and one of them had throwed his gun on the marshal. Walt Sanders thought of Catherine back home and their three sons, and he wondered what they would do if he was killed in this. What would happen to his family if these strangers gunned him down in the Dry Gulch?

These thoughts all passed through Marshal Walt Sanders' mind in an instant, and they were expunged just as fast when more shots erupted in quick succession. The other two strangers at the front of the saloon both drew guns, but neither of them fired.

The stranger in the back of the Dry Gulch did all the shooting.

Marshal Sanders watched as the two men at the front of the Dry Gulch collapsed. Both men dropped their guns. The man farthest from Sanders clutched at his stomach. "Damn! I'm shot!" he called out. He dropped to his knees, whimpering. "Gut shot! I'm gut shot!" He cried out once or twice, but then went silent.

The man in the center never uttered another word. He stumbled backwards out of the saloon, turned, and fell face first into the dirt in the road.

Lodero shot and killed all three of the men.

In the immediate aftermath of the shootout, Walt Sanders tried to put together everything he'd witnessed.

Walt asked to see a warrant, and the man closest to him, the one he'd been talking to, he threw his pistol first. Marshal Sanders had no doubt about the man's intention. He was gunning for the marshal.

When that man drew, Lodero at the back of the saloon drew and shot first.

The other two men threw guns right behind the first, and they were both gunning for the stranger in the back. But Lodero fanned his pistol and rapidly got off three, maybe four, more shots. Walt Sanders tried to count the shots. Maybe five shots total -- but Lodero had fanned the gun so fast, Walt could only remember hearing three shots, including the one that took down the man who'd turned on him.

"What the hell just happened?" Wayne McClellan asked.

Walt Sanders turned to Lodero. Walt's hand was still on his revolver. The revolver was still in his holster.

"Don't throw that gun, marshal," Lodero said, and for a man who had just gunned down three men, his tone was mighty calm. "I got no quarrel with you, and I reckon I don't care much to shoot a lawman. But if you think I ain't walking out of here and riding on, you're sore mistook."

"You just shot three men dead right in front of me," Marshal Sanders said. "I can't let you just leave."

"That first one was throwing down on you," Lodero said. "If I'd not shot him, you'd be breathing out your last right now. He had the drop on you. Them other two throwed guns as soon as I shot the first. All three of them killings was self-defense -- yourself and my own self -- and you know it."

"But I can't let you just walk out of here," Walt Sanders said again.

"I reckon it wouldn't make you feel any better about it if I shot you dead and then walked out," Lodero

8

said.

Walt Sanders thought of Catherine and the children. Lodero had not holstered his gun. How many shots had he fired? Did he have one or two shots left in that six-shooter? Was he the sort who rode with an empty chamber? He might be pointing an empty gun. Could Walt throw his gun before Lodero could draw second gun?

Lodero stood steady as a rock. Marshal Sanders had fought Indians and Yankees and outlaws, and he'd seen plenty of killers in his day. But there was something about the cool, steady man in the black hat in the back of the room that unnerved him. Lodero spoke again, "All you have to do is say it was self-defense, justifiable killing, and they's witnesses can attest to it. Say it out loud, and I'll walk out of here and never come back. But more important to you, marshal, you'll walk out of here."

Marshal Sanders looked at the other men in the saloon, all of them over by the bar, all of them looking at him to see what he was going to decide.

"Hell, Walt, it sure looked like self-defense to me," Wayne McClellan said. "He's right, that fellow was drawing his iron to shoot you. No doubt about that. And them other two was going to shoot this stranger here. There ain't no shame in calling it what it was and lettin' this feller go."

Dale Burton nodded his agreement. "Marshal, it looked justified to me, too. Hell, the fact is, this stranger saved your life."

Walt Sanders knew that this was a decision for a judge and jury, but he had no doubts about the resolve of this man who called himself Lodero.

"It was defense of another and self-defense," Walt

9

Sanders proclaimed. "These shootings was justified, and I suppose I owe you my thanks."

Lodero spun his revolver and dropped it down into his holster.

"I'm sorry about bringing this trouble to your town, marshal," Lodero said. "I just wanted a meal."

Lodero walked easily to the front of the saloon, stepping past two of the men he'd shot. He walked out the door, deliberately stepping over the body of the man in the street, and crossed the thoroughfare to the livery.

None of the men inside the Dry Gulch Saloon said a word. None of them moved. A thickness had come into the air that had nothing to do with the dust nor the heat. Walt Sanders realized his heart was thumping hard inside his chest, so hard it seemed it might burst right out.

"My God!" Wayne McClellan exclaimed. "I ain't never seen nothing like that."

"Me neither!" one of the cowpunchers said. "Oh, my Lord, I ain't never seen nothing like that. How fast was he?"

"He killed all three of those men," Dale Burton said. "They was dead before I even knowed who was shootin'."

A few minutes later, Walt Sanders saw Lodero ride out of the livery on a fine black stallion with a white star on its face.

"Somebody run down and get Wes at his shop. Tell him he's going to need to make three caskets," Sanders said. "I hope I never see that man again as long as I live."

2

Lodero rode fast out of town. He should not have gone there. He knew those men were trailing him, but he hoped they would have given up by now. He rode at a gallop for a short distance and then slowed the stallion to an easy trot. After a bit, he recognized the rocky outcropping he'd been looking for and turned off the road. He slowed the stallion to a walk. Too many loose rocks to ride fast through here, and there was no trail. Just rocks and dirt and squat mesquite that tore at the tails of his duster when he brushed up against them. Everything here was flat countryside and low hills. It was not so different from home, but he preferred the Hill Country down south, the big trees, the flowing rivers, the green vegetation. He'd ridden through a valley there and decided if he ever came back to the Hill Country he might like to stay. He'd never seen so much green in all his life. By the time they got to Fort Concho, the terrain had leveled out and turned dry and dusty again, though a good river ran near the fort.

The smell of smoke let Lodero know he was close to the campsite. He and the stallion pushed through the mesquite, up a rocky incline and there below was the arroyo -- just a dry gully now, dry dirt like everything else around here. And down in the arroyo reclined the familiar form of the old Tejano.

Juan Carlos Baca was asleep near the campfire. His pretty bay horse was on a long tether staked to the ground. The horse snorted as Lodero and the black approached.

Baca did not move, his sombrero covering his face, but he spoke through the hat.

"Did you find what you were looking for, señor?" Baca's accent was heavy with his Mexican heritage.

Baca was an old man now, and had grown almost as round as he was tall, though he was not tall. He was not built to travel like this, and Lodero wondered if he should have left the old man at home.

"I did not," Lodero said. He had gone to town to see about finding work, at least for a few days. "But those three men who were trailing us, they found what they were looking for."

Still Baca did not stir. "You keeled them?"

"I did."

"Good riddance, too," Baca said. "We go on with no more looking over our shoulders. You should have left eet alone at the fort. That was not your concern."

Lodero swung himself out of the saddle. He unbuckled the saddle and removed it and the blanket and the rest of the tack. He thought about Fort Concho, about what he had done there. It was not the first time he had shot and killed a man, and he had no regret over it. The man deserved killing.

"I warned him to leave that woman alone," Lodero said. "He got what was coming to him."

"Maybe so," Baca said. "But eet put his brother and those other two men on us. If you do not want to be pursued, señor, you should not get involved in sech things."

Lodero untied the holsters from his thighs, unbuckled the gun belt and hung his Colt Peacemakers on a mesquite branch.

"I would have brought you some supper, but I left in a hurry."

"No matter," Baca said. Baca stirred and lifted the sombrero from his face. He sat up and put the wide hat back on top of his head. "Señoritas will be your ruina, Lodero. I just hope you do not ruin me as well."

Lodero rolled a cigarette and lit it from a burning stick in the fire.

"We are out of money, Juan Carlos. We should find work, but not here. Tomorrow we will ride on, and maybe in the next place we will find work."

Lodero took a seat on the ground near the campfire, though not so close that he felt any of its heat. It was too hot to sit close to a campfire.

"We do not need money," Juan Carlos said. "We are free men, Lodero. Unencumbered by the things of this world that hold men like slaves to their jobs."

Lodero shook his head and smiled at the old man. "Money is freedom, Juan Carlos Baca. A rich man goes where he pleases and does what he wants. He has the liberty to live his life however he chooses. A poor man is staked to the ground like a horse on the plains, forever working for his next meal. It was freedom my father sought all those years ago when he left home."

Juan Carlos shrugged. "Maybe eet is so, Lodero. A rich man is free, but we are poor men and we go where we want."

"We will go there hungry if we do not find work so that we can afford a meal."

"Maybe we should rob a bank, amigo."

"A hunted man is no more free than a poor man," Lodero said. "We will find work, enough that we can afford a little freedom."

Juan Carlos Baca was indifferent to work. He would work if he had to. His concern was only with the young man. His association with Lodero began before the boy was born, and it would not end until one of them was in a grave.

Lodero smoked his cigarette. He was quiet.

"It is a shame that a man should be so good at something that he hates so much," Juan Carlos said.

Lodero nodded thoughtfully. "No one has ever accused you of being good at work, Juan Carlos," Lodero said. He grinned at his old friend, but it took Juan Carlos a moment to get the joke.

"No, señor. You are very good with your guns, but eet troubles you to use them. No?"

Lodero flicked the end of his cigarette at the fire, watching the smoke curl away from it as it sailed through the air.

"Today I killed a man whose brother I killed. If their mother is still alive, I have stolen two sons from her. And I have stolen sons from the mothers of those other two men who I shot today. It is no small thing to cause women grief, and I am sorry for those mothers."

"Bah!" Juan Carlos spat. "If the mother does not want her son killed, she should raise him not to beat on señoritas and try to rape them. And those three men today, if you did not kill them, would they have killed you?"

"I reckon that's why they followed us so far," Lodero conceded. "They was coming to kill me."

"Do not grieve, then," Juan Carlos said. "They gave no thought to your mother when they rode after you."

"My mother is dead," Lodero said.

"Those men did not know that. And your seester would mourn for you. So those men gave no thought to your seester."

"They should not have come after me. They should have stayed at home," Lodero said.

"Si," Juan Carlos agreed. "They should have stayed at home."

Lodero shut his eyes and tried not to think about the men he had shot nor their mothers. He regretted killing those men, even though they gave him no choice. He did not regret killing the man at Fort Concho. That man had beaten a woman and tried to violate her in one of the stalls at the livery. That man earned his killing.

Thinking about the incident at Fort Concho naturally brought to Lodero's mind the memory of the first man he shot and killed.

The first man Lodero killed had also tried to violate a girl. It was so many years ago, in his home village. The

Comancheros had come to town and were getting drunk at the saloon. Everyone knew to stay off the street when the Comancheros came to town. Vile and filthy brutes. A lawless band consisting of Mexicans, Indians, and white men -- making their way on the very edge of civilization. Rape was nothing to them. It was nothing to them to take a white girl and trade her to the Comanche, along with guns and whiskey. And from the Comanche they would buy Indian girls or Mexican girls stolen in raids on ranches south of the border, and the Comancheros would trade them to white men for whiskey. When the Comancheros came to town, they were vicious and cruel, and everyone knew to stay off the street.

But Lodero's sister Sophia had run from their home into the street. She had gone for her dog, knowing the Comancheros might shoot the animal for sport. She was young and foolish, but she was older than Lodero and should have known better.

This was after their father had left the village. There was no one else who would protect Sophia. When Lodero saw the fat and dirty man with the heavy beard grab his sister by the arm and drag her, Lodero knew he was the only one who would risk his life to save his sister. He fetched from the drawer his father's Paterson revolver, the five-shot pistol his father had used in the war with Mexico. Before he left, Lodero's father had let the boy load the lead balls into the gun, place the caps on it, and with a promise never to tell his mother, Lodero's father had, a few times, allowed the boy to shoot the heavy revolver.

When he saw the Comanchero take his sister, Lodero loaded the gun with just one cap and one ball. He did not take more time than that. And he rushed from the house with the heavy Paterson in his hand.

He found the Comanchero with Sophia behind the saloon. The fat man who stank of whiskey and sweat had pinned her to the ground, had torn her dress to expose her.

Lodero ran right up to the man. The Comanchero was intent on his victim and never saw Lodero, even as the boy pressed the barrel of the Paterson to the man's head and pulled the trigger.

What a terrible thing. The gore was horrendous, and Sophia's screams still rang in his ears. But Lodero had saved his sister from being fouled by the filthy Comanchero.

That day, more than any other, he hated his father for leaving. His father should have been there. Their father should have been there to protect Sophia.

Their mother feared reprisals from the Comancheros when she learned what Lodero had done. She loaded the Paterson and hid Lodero and Sophia under a bed. But the Comancheros spent the night drinking and shooting their guns and yelling so that no one in the village slept. And in the morning the filthy brutes slept, and in the afternoon they left, and the body of the man Lodero killed was buried by Juan Carlos Baca and some of the other men in the village.

When the Comanchero was hidden in the ground, Juan Carlos Baca came to Lodero to talk to him.

"You are your father's son, Lodero. I knew your father for many years, even before your mother knew him. He was strong and brave and always did what he knew was right to protect people who could not protect themselves. You saved your seester just as your father would have done. You are the man now, in your father's place."

With the words from Juan Carlos, Lodero stopped

hating his father.

The memories turned to sleep and the sleep brought dreams of an empty trunk, and in the morning Lodero and Juan Carlos Baca rode on away from that arroyo.

3

Lodero and Juan Carlos Baca rode north for two more days before coming to a small town surrounded by cattle ranches. A thick layer of dust covered every building in the town. The long, dry summer needed rain to bring it to an end. The afternoon showers that typically blew up in the summer had been largely absent this year. Everything was dirty, including Lodero and Juan Carlos Baca. They rode slowly into the town -- past the livery with its horses all out in the corral while a couple of boys put down fresh hay in the stalls; past the sheriff's office and jail where a man with a tin badge dozed in a chair out front; past the hotel and the saloon attached to it, both quiet; past two other saloons, one of which had two men standing outside; past the several stores that all seemed empty of customers. Only a few people were on the street to take notice of the two strangers riding into town. This was a quiet town, built near the confluence of two small rivers that ran dry three months out of the year. Those rivers now needed rain.

A man driving a wagon loaded with supplies gave Lodero and Juan Carlos a long look as he rode past, but he tipped his hat, friendly enough.

"This is a quiet town," Juan Carlos said. "There will be no work here."

Neither man had eaten in more than a day. Juan Carlos felt a terrible gnawing in his stomach each time it rumbled.

Lodero had only a few coins left in his pocket. He turned the black stallion toward one of the saloons, swung himself out of the saddle and hitched his horse. Juan Carlos followed his lead.

"Free lunch with whiskey," the bartender inside the saloon said. A buffet table was set up against the wall opposite the bar.

There were two men seated at a table near the bar, both with plates and whiskeys in front of them. They looked like businessmen. Their suits were not covered in dust like everything else. Their clothes were clean. There was no dirt around their fingernails. Their beards were neatly trimmed.

"A whiskey for my friend and me," Lodero said, giving over the last of his coins to the bartender.

"He'p yourself if you want some lunch," the man said.

Juan Carlos went for the buffet table. Lodero waited a moment.

"We're looking for work," Lodero said.

"What kind of work?" the bartender asked.

"Anything. I'm good with horses, but we need to find something."

"Ain't much around here," the bartender said. He

20

glanced at the two men seated near the bar. They were paying attention to the conversation. "Only one I know who might be looking for hands is the Widow Noble. She's got a ranch about twenty miles from here off the road going north. It might be worth your while to ride up that away."

"Much obliged," Lodero said. He started to take his whiskey and go to the buffet, but one of the men seated at the table spoke up.

"You'd be wasting your time to go up there to the Noble place, friend," he said. His tone was friendly enough, and he said it with a smile. Still, there was something to the man that Lodero did not trust. In his home village there had been no banks, no stores, no businessmen in clean suits. Lodero grew up in a hard scrabble village near the border with Mexico where chickens roamed the streets and freighters passing through sold the only goods the villagers ever saw and Comancheros sometimes came to the village to drink at the only saloon and rape and kidnap women. So Lodero's experience with men such as this was not extensive, but his experience with men who could not be trusted was as vast as the desert.

"Why do you say that?" Lodero asked.

"I'm just trying to save you some time, friend," the man said. "The Widow Noble -- her husband died in the spring and she missed getting her stock on the cattle drive. The trail boss couldn't wait for her. She has land, and she has stock, and she may well have jobs that need done, but she ain't got no money. Another couple of months, and the Widow Noble will have to sell that ranch and all her stock."

"Thank you for the information," Lodero said.

"I'm glad to help you, stranger," the man said. "I just hate to see you waste your time. If you're looking for work, best thing to do is ride on east of here, over to Jacksboro or north up to Wichita Falls. Plenty of work in those places."

Lodero nodded his head to the man and joined Juan Carlos Baca at the buffet table. They both piled their plates high, and Lodero dropped a couple of biscuits into his pockets to have for later. They took a table away from the others in the saloon.

"Did you hear all that?" Lodero asked Juan Carlos. He spoke softly so that the men at the other table would not hear.

"I hear," Baca said. Juan Carlos did not have a soft voice. "It does us no good to work for a widow who cannot pay."

It was true, of course. They were out of money and hungry. A job was no good if there was no pay. But it might be that the widow could feed them, and maybe give them food to take if they worked for her for a few days. The alternative was to ride east to Jacksboro, but Lodero believed his destiny was in another direction. Silver City, New Mexico Territory.

"The man at the table recommended we go east to find work. That is the wrong direction."

"We will find no work for many days if we go west, amigo," Juan Carlos said.

That was true. West was the Staked Plain, the Llano Estacado, and there was nothing but rogue Comanche and Apache to the west, murderous Indians who had left the reservations.

Lodero kept his voice low. "We will ride north to the widow's ranch. Let her tell us that she cannot pay us to work."

Juan Carlos Baca shrugged. He was along for the ride and would not question Lodero's decisions. Lodero wondered, when Juan Carlos looked at him, if he saw the boy from the village or if Juan Carlos saw his old riding partner, the man who'd fought with him against the Mexicans as a Texas Ranger.

***

The two men rode north for several miles when at last they came to what they assumed was the Noble Ranch. There was good water on the ranch, a creek that was not completely dry this time of year was a rare thing. There were short mesquite trees and scrub oaks along the banks of the creek, and there was grass enough for grazing a good herd. Across the open plain, they could see hundreds of cattle on the land. And off the road, they could see the ranch house, sitting on a rise under a few tall cottonwoods with a grove of Texas persimmon trees nearby. There was a stable and corral out back, as well, and a smokehouse. The ranch house stood two stories high with white painted boards on the outside and many windows, all now open for the breeze. There was a windmill standing over a well near the house, and as he looked out across the horizon, Lodero could see a couple of other windmills.

"Eet is very pastoral here," Juan Carlos Baca said.

"Not as pretty as the Hill Country," Lodero said, though in truth it was one of the nicest spreads Lodero had ever seen. Everything about the home place spoke of wealth, and Lodero could not imagine a widow living here who could not afford to pay ranch hands.

"No, but much nicer than home," Juan Carlos said.

Lodero urged the stallion forward, and Juan Carlos followed him as they rode down toward the ranch house.

They were about half way to the house when they heard some shouting coming from the barn, and in a moment, a tall Negro came running out from the barn. He was yelling something that neither Lodero nor Juan Carlos could hear. What they could see, though, was that the man had a carbine in his hand.

"Y'all just hold them hawses right char!" the man yelled as he neared them, and he raised the carbine up to his shoulder as he continued to walk forward. "I ain't want to shoot ye, but I will do it if you keep on a-comin'. Miss Maria done tolt y'all to stay off dis 'ere ranch, and I'm to shoot ye if ye keep on comin'."

Lodero raised his hands up in the air.

"We're here to see the Widow Noble," Lodero said. "No one has told us to stay away from here. We were told in town the widow might have work."

The big, burly black man -- who wore the yellow-striped, blue britches of the cavalry and a cavalry hat -- kept the carbine pointed at Lodero and Juan Carlos, but he looked around the barrel at them, sizing them up.

"Who in town would have told you we had work out here?" he asked.

"A bartender in one of the saloons. I did not get his name."

The black man gave a knowing smile. "Well that would be Sammy," he said. "Sammy's a good man. He'd send ye up here. You ever worked a cattle ranch before?"

"We've worked with cattle some," Lodero said. It was a lie. "I'm better with horses."

The conversation continued to be carried across the

24

barrel of the Negro's carbine. But his tone had turned softer, and he was smiling now. He was a big man, tall with broad shoulders. He wore heavy leather gloves, and everything about his appearance suggested that he was accustomed to working hard.

"We ain't got no hawse work, but they's plenty around here that needs doin'."

"We're passing through," Lodero said. "We do not intend to stay long. But we need to earn wages."

The black man nodded. "That's for Miss Maria to talk to you about. Y'all ride dem hawses on down to the barn. I'll go an fetch Miss Maria, and she can decide if she'll have wok for ye here."

The man lowered his carbine and set off toward the ranch house. Lodero and Juan Carlos rode to the back of the house down to the barn.

"He thought we were someone else," Juan Carlos said.

"Clearly," Lodero responded.

"Does eet not worry you, señor?" Juan Carlos said. "He came at us with that rifle because he was expecting someone who should be greeted with a rifle."

"What worries me is whether or not we'll have supper tonight," Lodero said. "Whether or not we'll have breakfast in the morning. That's what worries me."

"Es una mujer anciana," Juan Carlos said. "What does an old woman know about ranching? They told us in the town that she missed the cattle drive. If she cannot pay us wages, we are wasting our time, amigo."

"Quit grumbling, old man," Lodero said. "She may

be an old woman, but maybe through her age she knows much about cattle."

They did not wait long before the Negro came from the back of the house and walked down to the barn. His gun was now down at his side.

"My name is Washington Scotland," the black man said. "Folks just call me Warsh."

"I am Juan Carlos Baca, and this young man is Lodero. We are up from a small village down near the border."

Both Lodero and Juan Carlos dismounted from their horses and shook hands with Wash.

"I guess I ought to apologize for coming at ye with the gun raised. We've had some trouble makers out to the ranch, and I thought you was more of dem."

"What kind of trouble do they make?" Juan Carlos asked.

"Rustlers, mostly. We got too many cattle, and folks know it. Old Man Noble died in the spring, and we missed the cattle drive. So dey's too many cows. And we've had some trouble getting hands, so dem cows is spread all out hither and yon. Easy for rustlers."

Lodero believed Wash was not being completely forthcoming.

"Do rustlers generally ride up to the front door of the ranch so that you can greet them from the barn?" Lodero asked.

"Ah, hell," Wash said. "No, I reckon dey don't. Whar is Miss Maria, now?" He turned and looked over his shoulder back at the house, but no one had come out.

26

"She'll be along shawtly."

"Maybe we should go up to the house so she doesn't have to walk so far," Juan Carlos said.

"Why's that?" Wash asked.

"The Widow Noble, being elderly, I thought she might not want to walk so far," Juan Carlos suggested.

"Her 'being elderly'?" Wash repeated, asking it as a question. Then he started to laugh. "Oh, I see what you mean. Yes sir, the Widow Noble can make it down that hill all right." He continued to laugh at his private joke.

But in a moment, Lodero and Juan Carlos were also let in on the joke as the back door to the house opened and the Widow Noble came outside.

Had he painted a portrait of everything most beautiful in a woman, Lodero could not have captured so true an image as that of the Widow Noble descending the hill from the ranch house.

Black hair and black eyes, her youthful skin kissed golden by the sun, her lips spread into a smile of gleaming white teeth. She wore a man's trousers and shirt and coat, all too large for her so that the cuffs of the trousers and sleeves of the shirt and coat were rolled up. But as loose as the clothes were, they could not hide the fine figure of the woman, round where she should be round and flat where she should be flat. She had long legs and long arms that suggested strong muscles under the shirt sleeves.

Maria Noble was not born to affluence. She was the second wife of Nicholas Noble, a wealthy rancher who died when he was sixty-two years old, more than twice her age.

As she came down the rocky hillside with plenty of

dexterity, she shattered whatever conceptions Lodero and Juan Carlos had about the widow.

And Lodero, for his part, found himself overcome by her beauty.

"I am Maria Noble," the woman said, extending a hand for them to shake. "You'll have to forgive my appearance. Wash and I have been branding calves this morning, and I've not yet had an opportunity to make myself presentable."

"Señorita, you are beyond presentable," Juan Carlos said, and Lodero believed the man's voice was suddenly deeper. "I am Juan Carlos Baca, and this is my young friend Lodero. We are up from the border, traveling, and when we were in the town we heard that you are in need of assistance on your ranch, and we have come to see if we might be of assistance to you."

"Señor Baca, you have come at the perfect time," Maria Noble said. Lodero noted that there was just the slightest hint of an accent, but her English was nearly perfect. "Mr. Scotland and I were just saying this morning that it would be mighty helpful to us to have another hand or two on the ranch."

"We are at your service, Mrs. Noble," Juan Carlos said, and Lodero noted that the old man was no longer talking about wages.

"I have to be honest with you. We missed the last cattle drive, and presently my funds are very short. If you stay on for the next cattle drive next spring, I will compensate you well. The next cattle drive will be in March, so about seven months. I would typically pay a hand twenty-five dollars a month, plus his spot in the bunkhouse and meals. But if you stay on until the next drive, I can pay you both two hundred dollars for the seven months. And, of course, you have the bunkhouse, two meals a day at breakfast and supper time, and you don't have to worry about feed for your horses."

"That ees very generous, señorita," Juan Carlos said.

"We may not be able to stay that long, but we'll take the thirty dollars a month if we cannot," Lodero said. There was something in the way Maria Noble looked at him that made Lodero feel like he had to explain. "We are traveling and are still well short of our destination."

"Where are you traveling to?" the Widow Noble asked.

"We're bound for Silver City."

"If you have come up from the border, are you not going out of your way to get to Silver City?" Maria asked. "Should you not have gone directly to El Paso?"

Lodero was reluctant to explain their travels, but he believed Maria Noble was reasonable in asking questions to know who she was hiring to work on her ranch.

"We left our border village and went first to San Antone," Lodero explained. "Then we rode to Fort Concho, and we fell into a bit of trouble there. Rather than ride directly to El Paso and then on to Silver City, we thought it best to go out of our way a bit, and so we came north."

"I see," Maria said. "And what sort of trouble did you have at the fort?"

"Lodero defended the honor of a woman who was being attacked," Juan Carlos said. "Eet ees his way."

"Do you have a streak of chivalry, Mr. Lodero?" Maria Noble asked. Lodero felt himself blush under her gaze. Her beauty baffled him.

"It ain't like that," he said.

"Oh, well that is a shame."

"A shame?" Lodero asked.

"This world needs more chivalry, Mr. Lodero. It is a shame if you cannot add to its store."

"He ees chivalrous," Juan Carlos said. "But he ees also bashful."

"The world also lacks in modesty," Maria Noble said, turning from Lodero back to Juan Carlos. "Perhaps Mr. Lodero can aid in the replenishment of both chivalry and humility."

"Si," Juan Carlos said happily, "and he ees also very good at reducing the numbers of the insolent and the prideful."

At the comment, Maria Noble's fell to the two Colt Peacemakers on Lodero's belt, but she quickly looked away.

"There are many insolent and prideful men in these parts, Mr. Lodero," she said. "I'll ask you not be too quick to unholster your guns when you are on my ranch."

"Oh, I have said too much," Juan Carlos said. "Eet ees not like that."

"You have not said too much," Maria Noble said. "I just want an understanding among us. I would like to avoid compounding my difficulties by adding gun play to them."

Maria cast her eyes to Lodero's face again. She silently prayed that her expression did not give away how much she was drawn to him. He was tall and very handsome with dark hair and light, gray eyes. His features looked etched from stone, and she could see that he had broad, strong shoulders, and his arms were lean and full of muscle. For just a moment, as she looked at him, she imagined him putting his strong arms around her and holding her tight against him. It would be a comfort to have a strong man to hold her. But she shook her head to dispel that thought.

"It is too late in the day to get started on any work. Put your horses in the corral, and Wash, you'll show them the bunkhouse?"

"Yes ma'am, I'll do it," Wash said. "Y'all come along with dem hawses and let's get you set up."

4

After they'd left their horses at the corral and given them water and fresh hay, Wash showed them down to the bunkhouse, a dugout with rock walls and a roof situated on the other side of a rise not far behind the barn. They had little gear beyond their guns, clean shirts and socks stuffed into their saddlebags and bedrolls.

"Y'all make y'selves comfortable in the bunkhouse," Wash told them. "The good news is the same as the bad news -- you've got the bunkhouse to y'selves. All the other hands done gone off, and I live in a little hut farther on down the ranch."

"Just you out there?" Lodero asked him.

"My wife and chillen live there with me. My wife, Junie, does the cooking on the ranch. We take most meals up at the main house. It's just Miss Maria up at the house, and so she eats with us. She works the ranch with me, too, now that the hands is all gone. Y'all gone be surprised to see how she works."

"What has happened to the hands?" Juan Carlos asked.

"We's had some troubles since the old man died," Wash said. "It ain't nothing to worry y'all. Dem other hands, they went for better wages on other ranches, some of 'em. Some of 'em just moved on to other places."

Juan Carlos Baca's stomach waged an audible war inside him. "Forgive me," he said, laughing at the noises emitting from his stomach. "We have not eaten today."

"Ah, hell," Wash said. "I'm sorry about that. I should have realized you boy'd be hungry. Y'all come on up to the house in about half an hour and we'll have supper ready by then."

They ate in the main house -- Maria Noble, Wash and his wife and two children, Juan Carlos and Lodero. Wash's wife, Junie, had made up a stew with beef, carrots, potatoes, and onion, and Juan Carlos Baca immediately pronounced it "not bad eatin'," though he did not add that he was hungry enough to eat saddle leather.

Maria Noble asked many questions about Lodero and Juan Carlos Baca, but Lodero did his best to divert her questions.

"Are the two of you related?" she asked.

"Lodero's father and I rode together in the war with the Mexicans," Juan Carlos said. "We were Texas Rangers and fought together from Monterrey to Mexico City. Now I ride with Lodero."

Maria seemed to want to ask about Lodero's father but could not find the polite way to ask the question. Lodero intervened.

33

"Wash, you wear a cavalry hat and britches. Were you in the army?"

"Yes, sir. I was up at Fawt Richardson for some years. My enlistment came up, and this old Buffalo Soldier decided to try his hand at wokin' on a cattle ranch."

"How does it compare to the army?" Lodero asked.

"I'll say this about it, in all them years I was in the army, dem Injuns shot back a fair few times. I ain't yet had no cow shoot at me."

"The village you come from, does it have a name?" Maria Noble asked.

"Eet ees so small, eet does not deserve a name," Juan Carlos answered. "We have a saloon and a few houses near the saloon, and that is all there is in our village. So we just call it 'the village.' If we get two saloons, we will give the town a name."

"Did you work together in your village?" Maria asked.

"Juan Carlos is just an old coffee boiler," Lodero joked. "He does not work. He supervises me while I work."

"Have I hired a man who does not work?" Maria asked, though she knew Lodero was only teasing Juan Carlos.

"It is okay," Lodero said. "I work enough for two men, and Juan Carlos will boil the coffee that keeps me going."

"Do you have a wife and children, Juan Carlos?"

"I am an old bachelor," Juan Carlos admitted. "I called on many girls when I was young, but I liked them all

34

too much to choose just one of them."

"And what of you, Lodero? Are you married? Do you have children? Or are you also a bachelor?"

"I am also a bachelor," Lodero said.

"But he is a young bachelor, and there ees still time for him to change his ways."

Juan Carlos Baca, in the past few years, had not laid eyes on a pretty girl that he did not try to fix up with Lodero.

After supper they parted ways, Lodero and Juan Carlos going off to the bunkhouse, Wash and his family going to their cabin, and Maria Noble stayed alone in the big house.

The late afternoon turned started to turn dark as they made their way to the bunkhouse, and with full stomachs, Lodero and Juan Carlos both were eager to sleep in their beds.

But before they fell asleep, Lodero told Juan Carlos what he had been thinking.

"She is familiar to me," Lodero said.

"Oh, amigo, you wish you had ever seen such a lovely woman," Juan Carlos laughed.

"No, I am serious, Juan Carlos." Lodero did not have to search his memory long to recall the face of a girl who had captured his imagination when he was young. "Do you remember the girl from the village? Rosita was her name. Does the Widow Noble not resemble her?"

"The Rios girl?" Juan Carlos said. "Rosita Rios. I remember her, but I do not remember so well what she looked like. It has been many years. Her parents were Tejanos. They left the village when her father died."

"That's right," Lodero said. "It was not long after I shot the Comanchero that she moved with her mother and her sisters. Or maybe it was before. I cannot remember. She was Sophia's age, two years older than me. Even as a boy, I took a shine to her."

"Perhaps, there is some resemblance." Juan Carlos said thoughtfully, "But I do not believe, Lodero, that it would be the same girl. She moved with her family back to Old Mexico where her mother had people. That girl would not be here living on this fine ranch."

"If I had a dollar, I would bet that Maria Noble is Rosita Rios," Lodero said.

"How long will we stay here, Lodero?" Juan Carlos asked. "Will we stay on until spring?"

"We will stay on for a month, Juan Carlos," Lodero said. "We have come too far to stop now. We will work for a month, earn wages here, and go on to El Paso after that. And then we will go to Silver City in New Mexico Territory."

Juan Carlos took a deep breath and let it out slowly, audibly. "And what do you hope to find there, amigo? I fear you will be disappointed."

"Answers," Lodero said. "I do not expect to find anything more than answers."

Juan Carlos Baca was indifferent. He would ride to El Paso. He would ride to Silver City. He would ride with Lodero wherever he wanted to go. But he was worried that his young friend was going a long way only to be disappointed.

"Some questions are not worth answering, Lodero," Juan Carlos said.

5

At dawn the next day, Wash Scotland met Lodero at the bunkhouse. Wash walked afoot with Lodero, leading his horse to the barn so that Lodero could get his black.

"It's odd to me," Lodero said, "that a man dies and his neighbors do not help the widow with the roundup. It makes no sense that Mrs. Noble would have missed the spring cattle drive."

"Deys a lot o' jealousy round 'ere," Wash said. "Mr. Noble, when he come out, he got the prime land. We got good water on dis ranch. Some of dem creeks run dry by the end of summer, but we got some year-round water. Most folks ain't so fo'tunate."

Lodero thought of what he knew of neighbors and their tendency to help one another in tough times. He wondered if Maria Noble's husband had been a difficult man. Lodero had worked for some horse ranchers, breaking broncos and driving horses to market. He'd never done anything like a cattle drive, nor gone those distances, and horses were easier than cattle because they were smart.

Cattle are dumb critters, and dumb is more difficult to handle. But the most successful horse ranchers Lodero met were always looking to undercut wages, always looking for a bargain. He understood that men who wrung the most value out of a deal often found success that others did not, but Lodero's preference was always to work for the modest ranchers, the ones who understood what it was like to try to make your way, who didn't bicker over wages or try to cheat a man.

"Our biggest problem right now is rustlers," Wash said. "They know we got too many cattle, and they come regular lookin' to steal. It's made worse, too, on account o' the water. Our good water is far out on the ranch, 'bout four miles to the east. That means it's easy fo' dem rustlers to get at the cattle."

At the barn, Lodero saddled his stallion, and he rode with Wash out across the ranch.

"We keep the herd on the ranch. They's grass enough, and good water, and Miss Maria don't want them to stray to the open range knowin' the way them rustlers is coming for her stock. We done lost twenty-five or thirty critters, maybe more. Missin' that cattle drive put Miss Maria in a real bind. She ain't got enough money to hold out here long, but if we can make the drive next spring she'll be put right. So now we just got to hang on to the stock we got, and hope them prices stay put."

Here on the far end of the ranch, the terrain was broken with deep arroyos, mesquite and scrub oaks. The grass was more plentiful here, and Lodero figured the stock had grazed heavily on the front pastures through the late spring and early summer.

As they topped a rise they came within sight of the

first of the stock they'd seen. Lodero figured there was something approaching a hundred head out in front of them.

"We got a thousand of dem cattle critters on the ranch, maybe more," Wash said. "Every rancher expects to lose a few to rustlers every year, but missin' the drive this year means we can't lose too many more. Next spring we've got to make up for this year and make our money for next year."

From the rise, Wash was able to point to the boundary of the Noble Ranch. "Beyond that deep arroyo there, that's the edge of Miss Maria's ranch. That's too deep and too steep for them critters, so we don't have them wander off from here much. They wander down at the south end of the ranch where there ain't no natural barriers. That arroyo is dry, so they don't have cause to want to wander down into there, and it's just as well. They'd fall and break their legs if they went down there. You can see farther to the north there, where them mesquite trees are in a line, that's a good year-round creek, and them critters will be all up along it.

As Lodero and Wash sat their horses on the ridge overlooking the stock, a terrible explosion of gunfire erupted from a batch of mesquite trees. There must have been a dozen guns all firing out their shells -- maybe as many as fifty shots all in quick succession -- and the men shooting off their pistols and rifles and shotguns went to hooting and shouting. The startled cattle started to move, pushing against one another, frightened and panicking.

"Tarnation!" Wash shouted. "They's gonna stomp!"

And sure enough, as he said it, the cattle started to make a run. The ground thundered with it and dust flew up in an enormous cloud, and just like that the cattle were in a stampede.

"They's making for the arroyo!" Wash yelled.

"Hyah!" Wash shouted, and the old Buffalo Soldier gave his horse spurs and together they were flying out across the plain, and Lodero watched with amazement at what seemed an effortless speed that Wash Scotland rode. He fit with the horse like a good, broke-in hat fits with a head.

The sun hit the thick cloud of dust and gave a golden glow to the chaos below. The thunder of the stock on stampede shook the earth. Lodero felt it in his chest.

Wash rode hard along to the far side of the stampede, his horse stretching at full stride to overtake the rush of the cattle and reach the lead cows. There was little room remaining from the head of the stampede to the arroyo by the time Wash reached the lead cows, little room for Wash to get the herd to turn. Lodero tried to judge if it was even possible, and if it was not, if Wash could not get them turned, he'd be bundled over into the arroyo with the stampeding stock.

Lodero felt his heart beating hard in his chest. He'd never before witnessed a cowpuncher mill a stampede. He'd not have known what to do even if he'd ridden with Wash. He was helpless up on the ridge, only able to watch.

Wash now had his lariat in his hand, waving it wildly. Through the sunlit cloud of dust kicked up by the cattle's hooves, Lodero could just manage to see that Wash was beating hell out of the lead cow with the rolled up, stiff rope. As hard as he could, Wash smacked the cow in the face over and over.

The distance from the front of the stampede to the arroyo was fast closing. Wash was shouting -- though Lodero could hear nothing of it -- and swinging the lariat, leaning far over to his horse's side to reach the cow. Now the lead cow started to veer to avoid the strikes from the lariat. Wash rode right beside the cow, striking it hard in the face, turning as the cow turned. It veered farther. The stampeding herd was following.

There was so much less space now, but Wash continued driving the lead cow, smacking it with the lariat until it was now turned so that it was running parallel with the arroyo. But Wash kept going, kept striking the cow's face. And now the lead cow was veering away from the arroyo, turning back the way it had come, and the stampeding herd was making the big arc with the lead cow.

Wash now turned away, giving off with the lariat and riding away as the lead cow turned full into the stampeding herd. The stampede was turned in on itself, and the cattle crowded in among each other, had stopped the stampede. All the run was gone out of them.

Wash and his horse had come out unscathed, but milling a stampede was dangerous work. Lodero knew of instances where cowpunchers had attempted to mill a stamp and they or their horses were trampled to death. The success of such a gamble often depended not just on the skill of the cowpuncher but also on the skill and training of the horse.

***

Seeing the stampede come to a halt and Wash come out the other end, Lodero now turned his attention to the thing he could do something about. He'd have been helpless to stop the stampede on his own, but he had skills that could still be of use.

He rode down off the ridge and rode hard for the clump of mesquite trees where the shots that started the stampede had originated.

He found numerous empty shell casings, some from rifles and others from revolvers. The men who had fired their weapons were gone, but they had reloaded their six shooters before leaving.

Lodero swung himself out of his saddle and examined the ground. The men had been on foot, and in the dry dust it was easy enough to follow their tracks. He went on about a hundred yards through the mesquite before he found a clearing where the tracks in the ground indicated several horses had been tethered for a while. The dust was kicked up all in the clearing and the rocks were chipped with white scuff marks. The trail where they rode away was well marked -- they had come in on the same trail they rode out on.

Lodero mounted his stallion and followed the trail out of the mesquite, down a trail into the deep arroyo, and out the other side. The tracks of the men who'd set the stampede were as clear as a road, and Lodero followed it with ease. They'd made no effort to disguise their presence. They'd made no effort to disguise their purpose. These men were not rustlers, neither, for their intention had been to stampede the cattle, scatter the herd and maybe -- probably -- kill the cattle that went into the arroyo. Rustlers gained nothing from dead cattle.

After some miles across the open plain, broken by dry creeks and low hills and mesquite, Lodero saw ahead of him several men on horses riding at a slow walk. He scouted out a path through the mesquite that would take him behind a hill and allow him to overtake the men without being seen. He urged the stallion forward and followed the new path around the backside of the hill, through the mesquite, and around to the trail the men were following.

He sat his horse in the middle of the trail and drew his Winchester rifle from its scabbard, and there he waited for the men to come down the trail.

"Howdy stranger," the first man said, riding up to him. The man was obviously cautious, and Lodero noticed that his hand was on the grip of his holstered pistol.

"I seen what y'all done there," Lodero said. "Settin' them cattle to stamp."

"You accusin' us of something?" the front man asked. They'd all reined in and were sitting their horses in the trail. The mesquite trees around forced the men to stay in a compact group on the trail and prevented them from coming out wide around Lodero.

"I'm tellin' you what I saw," Lodero said. "And now I'm givin' you fair warning. I've hired on at the Noble Ranch, and I've given the Noble widow a promise that her stock will make the drive come spring. If y'all come up on the Noble Ranch again, you'll be trespassin'. And here's your warning: I'll shoot trespassers."

"You're talking mighty big for one man against twelve," one of the men in the back said.

"You ought not to speak for these men up front," Lodero said. "They'll be the first to get shot from your talk. But don't you worry. If you give me cause, I'll work my way back to you."

The man in the front, with his hand still on the grip of his holstered six-shooter, spoke now. "Confident, ain't you?"

Lodero shrugged his shoulders. He did not boast about this. "I'm just statin' facts," Lodero said.

The man in the front moved his hand away from the grip of his revolver.

"We ain't here for a gunfight, anyhow. You've said what you came to say. Now let us pass."

Lodero whistled to his horse and tugged the reins, and the stallion backed away and onto the path he'd ridden to get around the men.

The man up front squeezed his horse and it started to walk forward. "My name's Jake Mullen," he said. "Who're you?"

"Name is Lodero."

Mullen was now even with Lodero. "I'll be seein' you again real soon," Mullen said.

"That's fine," Lodero said. "So long as it ain't on the Noble Ranch."

Mullen grinned, appreciating the fast quip.

As each man passed, Lodero watched them close, looking into their faces so that he would remember them. He did not want to encounter them unaware and risk getting back shot.

He'd taken a measure of them, too. There were a couple of them who looked him in the eye as they passed. These were men who wanted to convey to Lodero that they were not afraid -- his threats did not scare them and their body language was intended to let him know that they would be back. Most of them looked down as they rode past but gave him a sideways glance from under the brims of their hats -- these were men who would back shoot him given the opportunity, but they would never stand him up in a fight. The sideways glance was out of fear, these men were scared as they rode past. A single man chasing down and blocking the path of a dozen men was a man who was confident in his abilities with a gun -- or a fool -- and these men were worried it was the former and not the latter. They were good enough cowpunchers, but they were not interested in throwing guns with someone like Lodero. Mullen, though, rode on ahead with his eyes forward. He did not spare a glance for Lodero nor try to return an intimidating look. Lodero noticed, too, that Mullen wore two six-shooters where most of the other men carried only one, and Mullen wore them tilted forward in a quick-draw fashion rather than down on his hip like most of the cowpunchers. Mullen was a cool hand, and Lodero marked him as a hired gun. He was no cowpuncher and no cattle rustler.

When they were gone, Lodero rode back down the trail to the Noble Ranch. It was late in the afternoon by the time he arrived back. Wash was waiting on him up on the ridge, the one where Lodero had watched as Wash milled the stampeding cattle. But Wash was not alone. Another rider's silhouette was up on the ridge with Wash, both of them sitting on their still horses and watching Lodero as he came back along the trail through the mesquite and then into the open plain. The herd of cattle were still now, grazing haplessly as if no near-fatal event had taken place.

"Dem critters sho' is dumb, ain't they?" Wash called to Lodero as he rode up.

The second person on the ridge was Maria Noble, sitting astride a fine strawberry roan. She was wearing men's trousers and a man's shirt, suspenders and boots and a broad brimmed hat. Until closer inspection, she looked just like any other string-bean cowpuncher out on the range. On her hip was a six-shooter, and she had a Winchester rifle in a scabbard on her saddle.

"Ma'am, you've got yourself a real cowpuncher here," Lodero said as he rode up to Maria and Wash. "I've got to tell you, Mr. Scotland, I'm mighty impressed by the way you handled that stampede today. I ain't never seen nothing like it."

"We all gots things we's good at," Wash said. "I can ride herd pretty well."

"My husband always said that Mr. Scotland is the best hand he's ever seen on a ranch, and the best rider, too. That is why Mr. Noble made him the boss on our ranch."

"The important thing is thinking like dem critters, and then you can get them to do what they want. And cattle are some dumb critters, so I ain't gots to think too hard," Wash laughed. Like most men who worked with hard on the back of a horse, he didn't care too much for being praised. He was more comfortable chasing down a herd of stampeding cattle and turning the herd than he was sitting astride his horse and have folks talk about him in such a way.

"I was up on the north end of the ranch looking out for strays when I heard the gunfire," Maria Noble said. "I was too far to be of any help, and all the dust had settled by the time I got down here. But I found Mr. Scotland on the ridge here waiting for you to come back, and I decided I'd wait with him."

"Where'd you disappear to?" Scotland asked.

"I tracked the men who started the stampede," Lodero said.

"I figured," Wash said.

"I warned them to stay off the ranch. Told them they'd be treated as trespassers if they came back."

"Like I said, we all gots things we's good at."

"Man in charge was a fellow named Mullen. That mean anything to you?"

"I might have heard of him," Wash said, but he cast a glance at Maria Noble.

"They weren't rustlers," Lodero said. "They had no intention of stealing cattle. They were here to scatter and kill the herd."

"Naw. I reckon they wasn't rustlers," Wash agreed.

"I don't care what's going on here," Lodero said. "Juan Carlos and me, we signed on, and we're here. But we should know what we're up against."

Again, Lodero caught a glance between Scotland and Maria Noble.

"Let's ride this herd away from the arroyo, closer to the stream up north," Maria Noble suggested. "After we're done, Lodero, you ride to the house with me, and we will talk."

6

"My husband, Nicholas, has two sons," Maria Noble said.

She and Lodero were in the parlor of the big house. It was finely furnished with cushioned sofas and pretty knick-knacks. If he'd have put a word on it, Lodero would have called the parlor "dainty," because everything seemed fragile and small. The furnishings did not suit Maria Noble, dressed as she was in the attire of a cowpuncher. Petite though she was, and slender, Maria Noble had a force of personality that made her seem large, and dainty knick-knacks felt out of place around her. All the same, Lodero was self-conscious about the dust that came off him in a cloud when he took a seat on the sofa.

"They are from his first marriage. Both of them opposed his marriage to me. His first wife died several years ago, and Nicholas was a lonely man when I met him. His sons were grown and had moved out of the house, and outside of his cook and maid, Nicholas had no one to keep him company. This is back in San Antone. Nicholas had done very well there. He owned a supply store and had been there since before the war. He had a ranch and a big house and an interest in the bank. He was involved in politics, and had been for a time elected to some position. He was a very wealthy man, and there were many women -- let's call them 'suitable women' -- who could have been a second wife to him.

"But Nicholas fell in love with his maid. I was the maid."

"Did you love him?" Lodero asked, a tinge of jealousy nipping at him.

"I liked him. I would not say that I loved him. Nicholas was funny. He loved to joke and tell stories. And he was kind to me. He thought I was pretty, and he liked having a pretty young girl around. But of course everyone in his society disapproved. I wasn't one of the suitable women. I was Tejano. I was young. I was a maid. I was all things wrong for a man of wealth and status. So we married, but we did not stay in San Antone where so many people looked down their noses at me and whispered about the old man and his young Tejano bride. Nicholas built this ranch as a place where he could live out his old age in peace, away from gossip, away from his neighbors and his sons worrying him because they disapproved of the choices he made."

Her heart broke to think of the way her husband's friends and family abandoned him. So he wanted to marry a pretty young woman who would give him comfort and care in his old age -- Maria did not see what was so wrong with that. She still got sad when she thought of the cruel way his sons treated him in the last months of his life.

"His older son, Daniel, was not so bad. He still came to see his father sometimes, traveling to the ranch here from San Antone a couple of times a year. Daniel, like his father, was a banker and has done very well. But the younger son, Nick, he was ashamed that his father would marry a Tejano. Nick tried ranching back at San Antone, but his cattle took disease and he lost most of his stock."

Standing, Maria Noble stopped her story. She walked to a window and looked outside at nothing in particular. Lodero sat silently, watching her. The clothes were too big for her, the trouser legs were rolled up at the ankles. The shirt sleeves were rolled up. Everything was baggy. But she had cinched the trousers at the waist, and he could see the curves of her body. Lodero felt a deep attraction to her, and he thought of Rosita Rios from the village. He wanted to ask her, but he chose not to.

"When Nicholas died, his sons both came here for the funeral. My husband's will left the ranch and the stock to me. Both of the boys received money, but Daniel received the house in San Antonio. Nick was angry because he believed the ranch here should have gone to him and not me. Both Daniel and Nick have accused me -- even when my husband was alive -- of marrying him only because he was rich. And of course that is true, to an extent. I'd never have married a man that age who was poor. But I cared for their father -- more than they did. When he took sick, I nursed him. While he was dying, I stayed by his side. If he wanted to leave the ranch to me, he had just cause. I was his wife. He left me nothing else. The ranch house and its furnishings, the property, and the stock. He left me no cash, and he left me none of his investments."

Lodero was starting now to get the gist.

"So Nick is trying to drive off the cattle. You missed the roundup and the cattle drive in spring. You need the money to keep the ranch. He's trying to force you off the property."

"We did not miss the roundup through neglect. That's the story they spread in town -- that the poor, helpless widow couldn't even get her cows to the trail boss for the cattle drive. But they hired my ranch hands or threatened those who would not leave. Two of my hands were beat when they refused to leave. Wash Scotland is the only one who stayed with me, and they threatened him, too. But Wash does not scare easy."

Lodero heard anger in her voice, and he imagined the difficult times there must have been when ranch hands were beaten, threatened, and hired away. It must have seemed like her world was falling in.

"Nick is not alone," Maria continued. "The man who owns the ranch south of me was my husband's lawyer, Bradford Decker. He is the one who has convinced Nick to stay here, to not return to San Antone. We have good water on this ranch, and Bradford Decker wants this ranch to add to his own. Nick is his tool for getting this ranch. And because Decker was my husband's lawyer, he knows my finances. When my husband died, I took out a loan so that I would have cash to pay the hands and take care of immediate expenses. I expected to be able to pay it back as soon as the cattle went to market.

"Of course, that never happened, and Brad Decker knows all of this. He knows that by forcing us to miss the cattle drive we are barely hanging on, and he knows if he can scatter my herd before the next cattle drive, I'll never be able to repay the loan. The bank will foreclose, and Nick will be able to pay off the loan with the money his father left him. I am sure Decker plans to buy the ranch from Nick or steal it the way he is trying to steal it from me."

Maria turned from the window to look at Lodero.

"So that is my story, Lodero. This is why you have found me and my ranch in such dire circumstances. There are men who want what I have, and they are scheming to take it from me."

Lodero frowned at her. The injustice rubbed him raw. Lodero grew up in a hard scrabble village where people knew injustice. When he was young, he picked up his father's gun to defend against men who were strong and abused those who were weak.

"Did you hire me to ride your herd, or did you hire me to protect your ranch?" Lodero asked in a quiet voice.

Maria did not look at him. She dropped her eyes to his boots and stared at them. She could not face him when she made the confession.

"When you came to the ranch yesterday, Mr. Scotland had you wait down by the barn. He came in and told me there were men looking for work. He said he could see in your eyes that you are a serious man who can stand in a fight. He said you might not be much use on most ranches, but you might be the best hand for us at this time."

Now she looked him in the eye. "I confess, I see it, too. You have a deadly calmness in your eyes. If you are not a killer, you should be."

Lodero held her gaze, looking into Maria's dark brown eyes. He thought she had a deadly calm in her eyes, too, whether she knew it or not. He had his own confession, but he did not look away to make it.

"I am a killer," he said. "And when I know I am right,

I will stand up in a fight. So whether you hired me to ride herd and fix fences or you hired me to shoot men who threaten your ranch, you hired the right man. I will see to it that your cattle are on the spring cattle drive."

7

Juan Carlos Baca helped Lodero heave the ladder into place. It was early in the day, but Juan Carlos was already drenched in sweat -- his shirt stuck to him, the sweat rolled down to the end of his nose and dropped off, it was thick and cool in his mustache, and it stung in his eyes. He lifted his big sombrero from his head and wiped his forehead onto his sleeve.

"I am too fat to work in this heat, amigo," he said to Lodero.

Though lacking his friend's heft, Lodero was equally soaked through.

They had been on the ranch a month now. Mostly Juan Carlos did work around the barn -- getting fresh hay for the horses and running the horses, repairing broken tools that had been neglected when Nicholas Noble took ill. Lodero rode the herds most days, keeping the cattle from straying off the ranch and keeping them near the good water. It was an easy enough job -- in the heat the cattle were not inclined to stray far from the water. Mostly, though, Lodero was watching for rustlers in the employ of Nick Noble. There had been no more trouble on the ranch, but Wash Scotland was convinced this period of calm would prove to be a harbinger of troubles ahead.

Scotland usually rode out onto the ranch with Lodero, and the young man's respect for the old Buffalo Soldier grew by the day. Not only was he a good hand and superb rider, but Scotland had harrowing tales of fighting Indians, and he enjoyed sharing the stories.

Maria also spent most days riding the ranch. She had found great enjoyment in the freedom afforded to a cowpuncher, the freedom of riding a good horse out across open terrain. She could laugh at the jokes Wash and Lodero shared and listen to the war stories of a man who had many times fought Indians. She found herself fascinated by the lives men led, and envious. She had no interest in lying flat in a buffalo wallow and praying to God to be spared from the Comanche or seeing a fellow soldier scalped, but Wash's other stories of riding for days while tracking renegade Indians and chasing them back onto a reservation -- stories that did not involve killing -- sparked her imagination.

Scotland treated her like any other cowpuncher, though he was respectful toward her as he would be to a woman and as he would be to his employer, but Maria still felt a close camaraderie with Wash Scotland and with Lodero.

Today, though, Wash had ridden alone to check the stock and left Lodero with Juan Carlos to replace rotted boards on the roof of the barn. Juan Carlos Baca refused to climb the ladder, leaving the work of going up and down to Lodero. He did not mind. Lodero found any work better than that which had occupied his childhood. As a boy, he farmed a small plot behind his family's home. His family relied on the vegetables and beans he wrestled from the ground with little water and no good soil, but he also took some to the market on Sundays. When he was not farming, Lodero cut bamboo from the banks of the Rio Grande, and his mother and sister wove the bamboo into baskets that they sold.

These were poor chores, farming and cutting bamboo. Lodero's joy came in riding the horse his father had left him and in listening to Juan Carlos Baca talk of what it had been like to fight the Mexicans in '48. When he could get caps and balls for his father's gun, Lodero liked to shoot bottles, and Juan Carlos Baca would often shoot with him.

Farming and cutting cane, these were terrible jobs.

Lodero much preferred riding the ranch, roping stray calves and bringing them back to the herd. He even preferred the hot and difficult job of replacing boards on the barn. He despised farming, and so when Juan Carlos Baca objected to climbing a ladder, Lodero did it without complaint.

They worked through the morning like this, but at noon, Maria came out of the house and spoke to Lodero. She was wearing trousers and a man's shirt, boots and wide-brimmed hat and a gun on her hip -- her usual attire for working the ranch.

"I need to go to town for supplies," she said. "Will you and Juan Carlos hitch a team to the wagon for me?"

"Yes, ma'am," Lodero said.

"I'll ask Juan Carlos to drive me, but perhaps it would be wise for you to saddle your horse and ride along with us."

"Do you expect trouble?" Lodero asked.

Maria Noble knew her enemies far better than Lodero did. In his time working horses on ranches, he'd met many cowpunchers and ranch owners. He'd even known cattle rustlers and horse thieves. The lowest of all these men would never do harm to a woman. Only back shooters and curs would cause harm to a woman. But for all he knew, Nick Noble and the men working with him were backshooters and curs.

"I do not know what they might do," Maria said.

Lodero and Juan Carlos hitched two horses to the wagon. When Juan Carlos pulled the wagon around to the door of the ranch house, Maria Noble came outside. She had not changed clothes into a dress that would be more appropriate for a woman. Lodero was startled by her appearance.

"Did you not want to change clothes before going into town?" he asked.

"I am going to work, Lodero. Why would I want to change out of work clothes?"

"Yes, ma'am," he said. "No reason you should."

As Maria Noble climbed into the wagon and Juan Carlos got the horses going, Lodero chuckled to himself. The folks in town would think she was mad, and maybe she was a little. But Lodero admired the woman's strength of spirit. She did not shy from the demanding work on her farm. This, too, he found to be an attractive quality. In fact, everything about her was attractive, and the longer Lodero and Juan Carlos stayed on the ranch, the more Lodero felt drawn to Maria Noble.

The ride into town was a long but pleasant journey.

Away from the hot work on the barn, there was a gentle breeze and a slight cooling in the air. It was still hot enough, but gentler days of fall and winter were coming now. As they rode into town, they could see growing in the distance the finger-like lone, low mountain that stood over the town like a sentry. Below the mountain, flowing into a gorge, was a big spring that had been the cause of the founding of the town. The mountain itself did not hardly deserve to be called such. Other than one large rock face with a steep cliff, the entire mountain was a gentle rising slope, and on foot or horseback one would not even know they were rising considerably as they went up the slope. But it was a prominent in an otherwise flat landscape, and some in town took pride in their mountain, hiking to the top on Sundays for picnics.

The town was busy with activity. Many of the area ranchers had come to town for supplies, and that meant wagons clogged the main road, especially out front of the stores. Women in dresses and men in suits crowded the boardwalks.

Maria Noble drew several surprised looks from the menfolk, and most of the womenfolk offered disapproving frowns.

At the store, Maria gave a list of supplies to one of the clerks and asked Juan Carlos to see to the loading of the wagon.

She then led Lodero out of the store and down the walk.

"I am going to see a man in his office, and I need to meet with him privately," she said. She handed him a couple of coins. "Why don't you wait inside the saloon there, have a drink, and watch for me to come out. By the time I am finished, word will have spread that I am in town. If Nick is laying for me, he'll be waiting when I come out. I do not think he will try anything in town in the middle of the day like this, but we might gather some idea of his intentions."

Maria started to walk away, but she stopped and turned to look at Lodero.

"I have asked you before not to be too fast to unholster your guns," Maria said. "I'll repeat to you now that request. I have troubles enough without killings. Even if Nick attempts to provoke you with insults, will you keep your guns holstered?"

"You're paying the wages, Miss Maria," Lodero said. "I'll do what you ask me to do, and I'll not do what you ask me not to do."

Maria Noble went into an office with a lawyer's name on the shingle out front. Neither she nor Lodero noticed the man in the suit who was watching them.

Lodero went into the saloon across from the lawyer's office, and at the bar he ordered a whiskey and beer. The saloon was the same one he'd been at a month or so ago where the barkeeper, Sammy, had told him he might find work on the Noble Ranch. If Sammy recognized Lodero, he made no mention of it.

A minute or two later, Lodero watched through the mirror behind the bar as three men entered the saloon. He recognized one of the men. It was the same man who'd been in the saloon the day he first came to town. The one who told him not to bother to look for work at the Noble Ranch. With him was Mullen, the leader of the gang of rustlers who'd been out on the ranch and started the stampede. Lodero recognized the third man as one of them who'd been among the rustlers as well.

The man in the business suit wore the bowler hat on his head. He walked up to the bar and stood next to Lodero and ordered a whiskey. Mullen and the other man took a seat at one of the tables.

"Howdy cowpuncher. Remember me? I was in here the day you come to town looking for work." He spoke with a friendly, pleasant tone. Nevertheless, Lodero felt an implied menace, a tension lurking between them.

"I remember," Lodero answered.

"I understand that even though I told you not to bother riding out to the Noble place, you've hired on there."

"That's right," Lodero said.

The man made a tisking noise with his tongue and shook his head. "Seems strange that a man looking for work would hire on at a ranch where they can't afford to pay. What's the use of working where you can't make wages?"

"I guess whether or not I can make wages is up to the widow who owns the ranch," Lodero said.

"I reckon so," the man said. "How long you planning to stay on at the Noble Ranch?"

"You're asking a lot of questions for a man whose name I don't know."

"My name ain't important," the man said. "But I'm in a position to make you an offer that would be mighty valuable to you if you had the right answers to my questions."

Lodero tilted his head to the table where Mullen and the other man were seated.

"Those two with you?"

"They are," the man in the suit replied. "But they ain't no worry to you. Not now, anyways."

"What kind of offer are you making?" Lodero asked.

"You planning on staying here long, or you just passing through?" the man asked again.

"I told Mrs. Noble that I'd see her through to spring when they drive the cattle north. Then I'm on my way."

"You got places to be?"

"I'm looking for something," Lodero said. "And it ain't around here."

The man was silent for a moment, thoughtful. Lodero felt himself being appraised as the man looked at him in the wide mirror behind the bar.

"I'll give you two hundred dollars in cash money right now, and you ride on. Keep looking for whatever it is you're looking for. But you can have two hundred dollars to help you find it."

"That's a lot of money to buy off a cowpuncher."

The man in the bowler hat laughed. "Look, partner, you and I both know you ain't a cowpuncher. Oh, maybe that's what you're spending your days on right now, but you're what we call a gunslinger. You're a hired gunman."

"Nobody's ever bought my gun," Lodero said, and there was a dangerous edge to his voice.

"Okay, okay," the man said, raising his hands in a gesture of surrender. "But what about three hundred dollars to pay you not to use your gun? Three hundred dollars, and you ride out of here tonight."

"I told Mrs. Noble I'd stay on until spring," Lodero answered.

The smile dropped from the man's face, and his tone turned harsh.

"I said three hundred dollars," the man said angrily. "Three hundred dollars. Now, I don't know what Maria Noble has promised you, but she can't pay three hundred dollars. I know that. And ain't no cowpuncher working for three hundred dollars, neither. You say your gun ain't bought, but if she's paying you three hundred dollars, then she's hired your gun."

Lodero turned to face the man. "Is there a reason that the Widow Noble needs to hire a gunman?"

"Listen, cowpuncher, you and I both know that if you stay here things is going to turn bad up on that ranch. Them rustlers ain't gone to quit coming. They going to keep coming. And men's going to wind up killed. Them's the facts. Plain and truthful. The only thing that's going to stop men from getting killed is if you leave that ranch. Now you can leave, and leave tonight, with five hundred dollars. That's right. Five hundred dollars. More money than any cowpuncher ever seen in his whole life. Or you can leave in a box with nothing. But one way or another, you is going to leave that ranch. So make it easy on yourself. Take the money and run."

"Just so I know, are you Nick Noble or the lawyer Decker?" Lodero asked.

"My name is Brad Decker, but that ain't no concern. Do we have a deal?" His tone was gruff. His patience was gone.

"I'm headed back out to Miss Noble's ranch. I'll be

out there to protect her cows," Lodero said. "Just like I promised her I would be. And I'll say one more thing about it. If you don't want your men getting killed, you'd best not send them back out there again."

Lodero dropped the rest of his whiskey down his throat. He started toward the door, but halfway there he stopped and looked at Mullen and the other ruffian at the end of the bar. "If you boys value your lives, you'll find a new employer."

"I promise you I'm quicker," Mullen said from his chair.

"I reckon it's a fair chance you are," Lodero answered. "But I shoot straighter."

Mullen stood up from his table and his right hand slid to the grip of one of his six shooters. He did not pull the gun, and Lodero kept his hands by his side.

"I don't scare, Mullen," Lodero said.

"There's coming a day, Lodero, when I'll sling this gun," Mullen said. His eyes were steady and his voice clear.

"That's going to be a hard day," Lodero said. And deliberately, he turned to show his back to Mullen and Decker, and Lodero walked out of the saloon.

He crossed the street and stood on the boardwalk waiting for Maria Noble to come out of her lawyer's office.

8

Lodero staked the stallion in a patch of grass. While the horse ate, he reached into one of his saddle bags and pulled out a sack of tobacco and papers. Leaning against the horse with his elbows on the saddle, he rolled a cigarette. He had selected a spot on high ground where he could see out across the wide, north pasture where the cattle were grazing. This was the best grass on the ranch, not overgrown with brush. There was good water here, too. The fact that the high ground had a few tall cottonwoods where he could be in the shade added to his high opinion of the north pasture.

He stroked the stallion's neck and patted the horse.

A man's horse was everything valuable in this world. Without a horse, a man had nowhere to go. If he lost his horse too far from everything else, it could be a death sentence. Lodero knew horses, and he'd never seen a better one than this stallion. Lodero got the horse four years before while working on a horse ranch down near the border. He'd broken several broncos for the rancher, and in addition to his wages the rancher gave him his pick of the lot. The horse had been an enticement to come back, which Lodero had done a number of times. Stallions could be ornery, especially when a mare might be around in late spring or summer, but Lodero found they were pretty easy to deal with if you understood what motivated them. And Lodero understood what motivated a stallion.

The black, in particular, was as loyal a horse as Lodero had ever seen. He was rough on other riders -- he'd thrown Juan Carlos Baca the one and only time Juan Carlos had tried to ride him. But the black stayed calm and willing when Lodero was on his back. It suited Lodero that his horse wasn't easy for other riders. It might make horse thieves less likely to be successful if they should ever try him. He had a good endurance, and he could run like the devil. Whether he was running or chasing, Lodero was confident there were few horses that could outpace the stallion.

In these years that Lodero rode the stallion, a sense of each other had developed between the two of them such that Lodero looked on the horse as more a friend than a beast.

He named the horse Estrellada Nocturno for his coal black coat and the white star on his face, but usually he just called him "hawse." And Lodero had a habit of talking to the horse when it was just the two of them.

"You are a fine, good hawse," Lodero said, patting the neck and shoulder. "We've come a good long ways, but when these cattle are gone in the spring, we've got a long ways farther to go still."

As he took a drag on his cigarette, Lodero saw a rider coming toward him. Even from this distance, he recognized the slender form of Maria Noble atop her favorite bay. She rode well, and Lodero admired her skill as a rider. She was not like many women he'd ever known. She possessed a reserve of strength that reminded Lodero of his own mother. She accepted what was without complaint and dealt with the problems in front of her. Lodero wondered how many other widows, faced with agitators from the outside and the loss of all her ranch hands, would throw off the dress and don the garb of a cowpuncher and take up his work, as well. Lodero had never heard of a woman cowpuncher before. But he figured if his father had gone off and left the family on a ranch, his own mother would have become a cowpuncher. That was the sort of woman she was. She dealt with the problems in front of her.

"She is a striking woman, ain't she ol' hawse?" Lodero said. "She strikes a fine figure riding out across that pasture. Truth is, if I didn't have places to go, she'd be what would tempt me to stay."

Lodero and Juan Carlos Baca had been more than two months on the ranch, now. Two months of working on the ranch, keeping a watch on the cattle, and two months of almost daily parleys with Maria Noble. Sometimes they rode together, but often Maria would find Lodero wherever he was on the ranch. They would talk for a bit about much of nothing. Sometimes they would have sandwiches together. Maria often asked about Lodero's village or his family. She was curious to know all about him. He answered her questions in an off-hand way, pretending he had little interest in these frequent conversations, but the truth was that he ached for the moments when he encountered her out on the ranch. On those days where business kept her, or she did not find him, Lodero felt at sundown that the day had been wasted.

Maria Noble and the bay crossed the pasture at a gallop, and Miss Noble's neck glistened with sweat as she rode up to a halt at the top of the rise where Lodero was watching her.

"Whew!" she exclaimed, smiling brightly. "That was quite a ride!"

She dismounted in the easy way of a person long accustomed to the saddle. Her white teeth shone as she took out a neckerchief and wiped the sweat from her face and neck.

"I think it's cooling off a little bit," Maria said. "Not as hot as it was last week."

"I believe you're right," Lodero said.

"Still hot, but not as hot." She breathed heavily as she talked, but the smile stayed on her face.

Maria tied the bay's lead to a branch of one of the cottonwoods.

"You've found one of my favorite spots," Maria said. "There's a nice breeze up here, and the cottonwoods offer a good shade. I've always enjoyed riding out here."

"It's a nice spot," Lodero agreed. "Grass down there is good for the cattle."

Maria Noble was a busy woman. She fiddled with the saddlebags, she checked the straps on the saddle, she walked first one way and then another, taking a long gaze in different directions. Lodero leaned against his horse and watched her as if she was a curiosity to him.

"What is in Silver City?" Maria asked.

"I ain't sure," Lodero said. "I know what I hope is

there, but I don't know whether I'll find it."

"What do you hope is there?"

"Answers is all."

Maria chose not to pursue the topic. She felt Lodero wanted to keep Silver City private, and so she did not press it.

"You are very fast with your guns?"

"I ain't sure about very fast," Lodero said. "So far, I've been fast enough."

"Have you shot many men?"

"I've shot a few. I ain't never gone looking for trouble, but trouble has a way of finding me."

"Does it scare you to be in a gunfight?" Maria asked.

Lodero thought about the answer to her question. "I don't reckon I've ever been scared in a gunfight. There ain't much time to be scared, so I suppose I don't really feel much of anything at all. I just have to do it."

"What about in the moments before? Do you feel fear before it starts?"

"Not fear, no. I just watch the man. I watch his face and wait for that moment when he decides to throw down. Then I draw and shoot."

"How do you know you'll be faster than the other man?"

"Fast ain't everything," Lodero said. "Any man can pull a trigger quick. It's hittin' what you're aimin' at that counts most. So I just stay cool. I get my gun up as fast as I can, but it's the accuracy that really counts. And I've got a knack for hitting what I'm aimin' at."

"And how do you do that?"

"Do what?"

"Hit what you're aiming at."

"I've practiced a lot with the gun," Lodero said. "But you just have to feel the gun as a part of your hand. You point the gun the way you would point your finger. Thinking about it like that, and practicing, makes it easy."

"Juan Carlos told me that in the last town you were in before coming here, you shot three men who came after you."

"That's right," Lodero said.

"Surely to kill three men who are gunning for you, you must be fast."

"I reckon," Lodero said. "I just fanned the gun is all."

"Show me," Maria said.

Lodero shrugged. He looked for a target and settled on the trunk of one of the cottonwoods.

"Ready?" he asked.

Maria, her eyes wide with fascination, nodded her head.

Lodero flipped the thong loop off the hammer of his right hand gun and stepped away from his horse to face the cottonwood. He held his hands out in front of him, steady as a statue carved in marble. His eyes did not move from cottonwood trunk. He stayed fixed on his target.

"Say 'go,'" Lodero said.

There was a moment's pause while Maria Noble

looked at the gun thrower she had hired on. His tall, lean body spoke danger and strength and confidence. She wondered about the boy forced to murder on behalf of his sister. How did that boy become this man?

"Go," Maria whispered, and immediately her breath caught in her throat as Lodero's right hand dropped toward his holster.

As the barrel cleared the lip of the holster, Lodero already had thumbed back the hammer. Once clear of the holster, the barrel of the six-shooter was already up, drawing a straight line to the tree. The gun exploded in fire and smoke. After the first shot, Lodero held the trigger back, and his left hand fanned up and down on the hammer. He went so fast that two shots sounded like just one, and he put four lead bullets in the cottonwood, all within two inches of each other.

Lodero spun the gun on his trigger finger and the dropped the iron down into the holster.

"How many shots was that?" Maria asked, looking at the chewed up trunk of the tree.

"Total of five shots," Lodero said. "I fired one when I threw the gun, then four more by fanning it."

Maria went to the tree trunk and counted the slugs. The cottonwood was not be three or four inches in diameter, yet Lodero had hit it with every shot.

"I want to try," she said, her eyes with excitement.

Lodero pulled his gun and emptied the four spent shells from the cylinders. He took four cartridges from his belt and reloaded the Colt. He sized her up while he loaded his gun. She was a slight woman, but strong. She had physical strength with her internal fortitude.

"I'll show you," Lodero said.

He took her gun and emptied the chambers, dropping the cartridges down into a pocket. He stood beside her, close enough that he could smell that her hair smelled like flowers even though everything around smelled like saddle leather and dust.

"Hold your hands in front of you. When you drop your shooting hand, cross your left hand across your body."

He took hold of her wrist and slowly moved her hand down to the grip of the six-shooter on her right hip. Now he put her thumb on the hammer.

"Cock it back as you're drawing," he said, "and pull back with your elbow so that the gun comes out of the holster and is already aiming. Once the barrel is clear of the leather and pointing at your target, pull that trigger. But when you pull it, hold the trigger back and don't release it."

Maria dry-fired the revolver and held the trigger.

"Now with your other hand, you fan the hammer. Keep your hand taut and draw a circle with it. You've got to be careful to draw the hammer all the way back and release it."

Lodero put the cartridges back into Maria's gun.

She did it just as he showed her, but her movements were slow and deliberate and inaccurate. The shots came off with long stalls between each one, but only one hit the target.

"I'm not very good," she said sheepishly.

"I shot a lot of bottles back home before I got good," Lodero said. "If you practice, you'll get better."

Lodero took her gun from her and loaded it again.

"That's hard on a shooting iron," he said. "When I was a boy, half-busted guns was all I ever saw, so it didn't matter much to practice fanning like that. It's fast, and it makes a big noise and impresses folks that's watchin', but it ain't accurate unless you can shake hands with the thing you're shootin' at. If you're in a real gunfight, the better way is to be accurate."

Lodero turned again toward the cottonwood.

"Draw fast, but bring your gun up high so you can see down the barrel and really aim at what you're gunnin' for. With your other hand, wrap up your gun hand like this. That supports it. Then with your left hand, thumb back the hammer like this."

He went through the motion of thumbing back the hammer with his left thumb without actually doing it.

"You see how it's steadier and you can get a better aim?"

Now he dropped the Colt back into its holster.

"Say 'go,'" Lodero said.

Maria waited a moment, then said, "Go!"

Lodero brought the gun up. He did not shoot from his hip but held the Colt extended out in front of him, nearly level with his face. He gripped the gun with both hands, and his trigger finger on his right hand worked the trigger while his thumb on his left hand cocked the hammer. He fired four shots -- they were fast, but not as fast as when he'd fanned the gun. But shooting like this, able to look down the barrel and truly take aim, Lodero impressed her with a new feat. He shot four branches right at the crook where they grew from the trunk, and all four of the branches dropped from the tree. The first one had not hit the ground when the fourth started to drop.

"Speed ain't as important as hitting what you're shootin' for," Lodero said. "A man who draws for speed will miss, most of the time. But a man who draws to hit his target is the one who walks away."

"Most of the time," Maria added.

Lodero laughed. "Yep, I suppose that's right. I guess even a quick man can get lucky."

Maria suddenly turned to look into Lodero's face. Her smile dropped from her face. "Could you be compelled to not go to Silver City?" she asked. "I mean, if I wanted you to stay on here at the ranch, would you?"

"I like it here real well," Lodero said. "I like working the ranch for you. But me and Juan Carlos Baca, we set out for a reason, and I don't think I could be satisfied if I didn't see that through."

Maria nodded. Her face betrayed her disappointment.

"If I asked you to come back after you've found what you're looking for, would you do that?"

"Yes, ma'am," Lodero said. "I reckon I could be compelled."

***

After supper that evening, when Wash and his family returned to their cabin, Maria took out a bottle of whiskey and three glasses.

"I thought we might drink a few toasts," she said

74

merrily. "I sometimes gets lonely in the house here, and I thought maybe a few drinks and maybe some songs would be pleasant."

The trio drank to health and to cattle drives and to each other. Juan Carlos told stories about Lodero breaking horses, and every story concluded with a bronc flinging Lodero to the ground. Lodero was good natured about the stories, and never failed to add that Juan Carlos was busy brewing coffee any time a bronco went to bucking. Maria enjoyed the camaraderie between the two men and envied them for their friendship.

Taking a sip from her whiskey for the courage to ask the question, Maria said, "What do you want to do with your life, Lodero? After you've found what you're looking for in Silver City, what do you want to do?"

Lodero ran his thumb through his mustache to buy himself time to think.

"I do not know," he said. "I am good at working with hawses, and I like that real well. I suppose, if I could find a way to make it happen, I'd like to have a hawse ranch one day. Breed and work hawses and sell them."

"He ees better with his gun than with the hawses," Juan Carlos said. "But being good with a gun is only a way to make a short life. When you are good with a gun, men will come to find you to see eef they are better. And one day, one of them will be. Eet ees better for a man to be better with hawses than he ees with a gun."

Lodero took a drink but offered no response.

"We should have a song," Maria suggested.

"Do you have a geetar?" Juan Carlos Baca said. "I can play a bit."

"I do," Maria said, and she went into another room to fetch it. She returned with the guitar, and Juan Carlos spent a few minutes getting it into tune. When he was satisfied -- though Lodero was not convinced it was any more or less in tune than when he'd started -- Juan Carlos sang a song.

"Come, all you Texas Rangers,
And listen to my tale,
I'll sing to you my story,
And you better learn it well.
When I was just boy,
I climbed the cliffs of Monterrey,
Below the guns of Liberty,
I helped to win the day.

"I fought the wild Comanche,
And I crossed the desert sand,
Defending every village,
Down to the Rio Grande.
It was there my captain told me,
'Son before you sleep this night,
Make peace with God in Heaven,
For tomorrow we will fight.'

"And when the sunlight touched
The sky out to the east,
Captain said, 'Eat up, boys;
This may be your last feast.'
With howls that sounded deadly,
And cries that broke the dawn;
The Comanche fell upon us,
With lusty arrows drawn.

"I saw them Injuns coming,

76

THE NOBLE WIDOW

I heard them give the yell;
I looked at my good comrades,
And watched them as they fell.
The arrows filled the sky,
And them Injuns didn't miss,
And I wished to see my sweetheart,
For to give her one last kiss.

"The Rangers all fought bravely,
With our backs to the Rio Grande,
The battle raged for hours,
But then we got the upper hand,
And when the sun was setting,
And the battle we had won,
So many Rangers had fallen,
All dying with the sun.

"So learn from my sad story,
Be you friend or be you stranger,
A perilous life awaits
The man who becomes a Texas Ranger.
And if you have a sweetheart,
To weep and mourn for you,
Stay home with her, amigo,
You're among the lucky few.

"But if you must adopt
A life of ranging 'cross this land,
Then do it with the Rangers,
And a six gun in your hand.
You'll never know a sweetheart
And the love that she can give.
Life is short among the Rangers,
But, son, you sure will live.

"Yippie yippie yay! Yippie yippie yo!
Yippie yippie yay! With the Rangers I will go."

The widow Noble applauded vigorously at the end of Juan Carlos Baca's song, her vigor enhanced by the cups of whiskey she'd drained. The song was popular enough among old Texas Rangers, but Maria had never heard it before. Lodero had sung some of the parts along with Juan Carlos -- it was a song he'd heard many times because it was a favorite song for Juan Carlos Baca because it reminded him of his own time as a Texas Ranger.

Juan Carlos smiled and gazed through glassy eyes at his young friend and the beautiful woman.

"My head is so full of whiskey that my brain is having to swim," Juan Carlos said. "I should retire to the bunkhouse before I am so blind that I cannot find it."

As he walked out the door of the ranch house and stumbled down toward the bunkhouse, Juan Carlos was still singing, perhaps too loudly.

"So learn from my sad story, be you friend or be you stranger,

A perilous life awaits the man who becomes a Texas Ranger.

And if you have a sweetheart, to weep and mourn for you,

Stay home with her, amigo, you're among the lucky few."

At the end of the verse, Lodero and Maria could hear him laughing to himself.

"I recognize that particular laugh," Lodero said. "It is

the one he reserves for when he has stumbled onto the ground. I would wager he has tripped over a rock."

Maria smiled sweetly. "What about you, Lodero? Do you have a sweetheart at home?"

Lodero scoffed at the notion. "There is no sweetheart. I have Juan Carlos Baca to nag me and my old hawse to keep me company. What would I do with a woman?"

"Truly? There must have been women. You are too handsome for there not to have been women."

"There were women," Lodero admitted. "But none worth speaking of."

The widow Noble saw the redness flush his cheeks and knew she had tread into a conversation which made Lodero uncomfortable. She could not help herself but to tease him, and at the same time she was desperate to discover more, desperate to unveil the heart of the man she was growing to love. She believed it was there, beneath the stoic, mirthless visage, beneath the buckle of the gun belt, hidden behind muscle that enveloped the body. The dark-eyed stranger must surely have a heart, and there must surely have been a woman who made that heart beat faster.

"Never a woman who sparked your fancy? Never a girl who made you catch your breath?"

"There was one," Lodero confessed.

The widow Noble laughed and clapped. "Oh! Tell me, Lodero. You must tell me. Who was she?"

"In my village, when I was a boy, there was a girl who came from a good family. She was two years, maybe three years, older than me. She was Tejano, like Juan Carlos Baca and most everyone else in my village. As I said, she was a bit older than me, and she would have never noticed the boy who could not take his eyes off her."

"You are a man, now, and two or three years might as well be two or three days. Now she would take notice of you. What happened to her?"

"Her father died when we were still young, and the girl left the village with her mother and her brothers and sisters. I believe they moved to Old Mexico."

The Widow Noble's playful smile dropped from her face. Lodero's story rang familiar to her. "How long ago was this, Lodero?"

"Would have been a dozen years ago, now," Lodero said. "Maybe a year or two more than that."

Lodero did not even notice that the playful tone had gone from Maria's voice. He did not catch how serious she had become.

"What was the girl's name?" Maria asked.

"Rosita Rios," Lodero said.

At the name, the Widow Noble caught her breath and stood from the table. "I'm sorry Lodero," she said. "It is late and I am exhausted. Please forgive me, but I am going to bed now. You can find your way down to the bunkhouse?"

"Yes, ma'am," Lodero said. He did not understand why she was so suddenly troubled, but he stood as she walked from the room. When she was gone, he resumed his seat to finish his drink, and when the glass was empty he left the house and walked down to the bunkhouse.

Lodero undressed and climbed into his bed. It was a fine bed, nicer than any he'd ever slept on in his entire life. The mattress was soft and comfortable. The bed clothes were soft and cool against his skin. Juan Carlos Baca was snoring, but it did not keep Lodero from drifting off to sleep, thinking of Rosita Rios and the widow Noble.

9

Lodero pulled the reins on the stallion and let the big black dance for a bit in the road.

He stared as far off down his back trail as he could see. There was no rider, no dust on the horizon, no evidence at all that he was being followed. All the same, he had an uneasy feeling.

He had ridden into town to take a letter to the postmaster. When Juan Carlos Baca and Lodero left home to journey west, Lodero's sister Sophia had made him promise to write so that she would not worry. His letter was quickly penned and left out any details of any of the things that had transpired, and he only told her that he and Juan Carlos had taken work on a West Texas ranch to earn enough money to continue on.

While there, Lodero caught sight of Brad Decker and the gunman Mullen, and they both also noticed him. Before he had delivered his mail, Lodero saw Mullen ride off out of town on a gray sorrel, and it left him nervous that Mullen was up to no good. With no indication that anyone was on his back trail, Lodero was worried that perhaps Mullen was somewhere ahead of him, laying in wait to ambush. Short of finding a different way to the ranch, there wasn't much Lodero could do other than to stop frequently and scan the horizon, front and back, and hope that he saw Mullen before Decker's hired gun pulled a trigger.

Up ahead was a small stream. This was the best opportunity he would have before getting back to the ranch to water his horse. But there along the narrow river, all but dry and waiting for the rains to fill it back up, the terrain was broken and covered in mesquite shrubs high enough for a man to hide behind. Lodero let the stallion walk toward the stream, but he kept his senses tuned to any sign of ambush. He had a bad feeling, and wished now that Juan Carlos Baca had ridden with him. Two men could spot an ambush better than one. And Juan Carlos, though old and round now, had once been a tough fighter. When Juan Carlos rode with Lodero's father in the war against the Mexican President, the two men had been feared fighters. With other Texas Rangers, they had scaled mountains and stormed forts and snuck past pickets and blasted their way through Mexican encampments in the middle of the night. The stories Juan Carlos told were half true and half exaggeration, but the true half was impressive enough.

Lodero dismounted and drew his Winchester from the scabbard on the saddle. He left the stallion to drink.

Sitting up in the saddle he'd be an easy target for a marksman behind a mesquite bush. Down on the ground they'd have a harder time shooting him from behind cover.

He also kept moving, walking aimlessly and changing direction frequently.

There was no sign of trouble. No sign he'd been

followed. No sign of any riders ahead. But in his gut he felt a gnawing worry that he could not explain.

He'd seen Mullen ride out of town ahead of him. Mullen could have been going anywhere, that was true. But still, the gnawing worry persisted.

The stallion had its fill and wandered over to where Lodero was standing.

"What do you say, Estrellada Nocturno?" he said to the horse. "Are we surrounded by bandits or not?"

The horse gave no reply other than to press its muzzle in Lodero's chest while he scratched its head. Lodero stood with the horse for a few minutes, casting his gaze over what he could see of the countryside. Here by the stream they were down in a wide and shallow gulch, and Lodero could not see much in the distance. All the mesquite brush, the broken terrain, the rocks -- a man could easily be bushwhacked in this territory. Lodero's sense of unease grew by the minute. He was not sure if he had a true premonition of danger or if he'd merely spooked himself.

"Old hawse, I think we'd best keep moving."

Lodero slid the Winchester into its scabbard and was reaching for the saddle horn to swing himself up into the saddle when a movement from behind a mesquite bush across the stream caught his attention.

At first he thought maybe he'd just seen a deer, but a man stepped out from behind the bush wearing a fringed buckskin jacket.

Lodero's hand dropped like lightning to his holster, but he heard behind him the action on a rifle's lever.

"Don't let that iron leave leather, or I'll plug you

where you stand," a voice behind him said. Lodero recognized the voice as Mullen's. "Put them hands where I can see 'em."

Lodero raised up his hands.

Buckskin jacket now began to walk closer. The stream was so low that he was able to step from the bank to a sandbar in the middle and then to the other side without getting his boots wet.

"We have not met yet," he said. "You can probably guess who I am."

"Nick Noble," Lodero said.

"That's right," Nick said. "I'm Nick Noble. The namesake and rightful heir to that ranch you've been working."

"The way I hear it, your father left that ranch to his widow."

The worry was gone. The gnawing in his gut had vanished. Now that the moment was here, Lodero felt an ease come over him. He was now aware of other men moving among the mesquite, closing in on him, and he knew Noble had brought more men than Lodero could deal with. It was the not knowing that had made him nervous, the anticipation of the thing was worse than the thing itself, even when the thing itself was bad.

"You takin' up with her?" Noble asked. "Have you and that trollop turned my daddy's place into a hog ranch?"

"If you didn't have these backshooters with you, you'd not say that again to me," Lodero said.

"Backshooters?" Noble asked. "Oh, no, you've got us all wrong here. We ain't going to shoot you. Shootin' a man and leavin' him to die on the ground don't send the sort of message we're looking to send. And we do intend to send a message. Unfortunately for you, you are the messenger. We're sending the message to the woman who now has the ranch that should be mine. And we're sending the message to any fool cowpunchers around here who think they can take wages from her, including that nigger soldier."

As Nick Noble made his speech, Lodero was aware that men were moving in closer behind him. His attention was on those men surrounding and crowding in on him so that he did not even hear what Nick Noble was saying. Lodero did not know if the men had been laying in wait in the crooks and crannies of the gulch and behind the mesquite for some time or if they had managed to sneak up around him while the stallion watered. It was a point of pride for him that he hoped they had been laying in wait. Getting bushwhacked seemed better, somehow, than having a gang of men sneak up on him when he was watching for them.

"The message you're going to provide is to let my father's widow know that she can't hire enough hands to protect those cattle. There ain't no way that stock is going on the spring drive. No way. The message is that any time she hires a man to work her ranch and try to see those cattle onto the spring drive, we're going to hang that man from a tall tree."

Noble looked over Lodero's shoulder and nodded his head, and Lodero braced himself for what he knew was coming. Still, even though he knew it was coming, the stock of the rifle driven into the side of his head was a staggering blow. Lodero dropped to his knees, but as he did he reached for his guns.

"Grab his hands," Mullen shouted, and immediately Lodero felt arms wrapping around his arms, dragging him to his feet.

Estrellada Nocturno snorted and blew and stamped his hooves, but the men were now dragging Lodero away from the horse.

"Up the hill," Mullen said. "Get him up the hill to that cottonwood."

There was a man holding his right arm and another man holding his left. Lodero twisted and shook, trying to break free. They'd not disarmed him, and he knew if he could get to one of the guns he could put up a fight and maybe get away. If he could shoot one or two of them, the others might hesitate, and in their hesitation might be an opportunity for escape.

But now a third man came up and slugged him in the gut, and Lodero doubled over. But the men on his arms held him fast, and first one fist and then a second smashed into his face. The punches were powerful and rattled his head. Everything was a blur -- his eyes could not focus even as another fist caught him in the side, and then another in the other side. The man's fists felt like sledgehammers. Another blow caught him in the side of the head. Still the men on his arms held him fast.

Lodero kicked out at the man swinging at him, and his boot caught the man in the groin.

"Ooft!" the man shouted, and he doubled over and dropped to his knees.

The men on Lodero's arms both laughed and called out taunts at the man who'd taken the boot to the groin. Lodero tried to twist free, but they still held him fast.

"Get him up here. I want to be done with this," Noble called.

The men on his arms started to drag him up the rocky slope to where Noble and Mullen were standing below a cottonwood. As they did, they turned him enough that Lodero was able to see the two men waiting for him below a tall cottonwood, and he realized Noble had slung a rope over a high branch. The end of the rope was tied in a noose.

Lodero tried to catch his breath, tried to focus his vision. He didn't want to panic, but his head was clouded with a fog from the punches he'd taken.

Even as the men continued to drag him up the slope toward Mullen, Noble and that noose, Nick Noble was coming down to meet him.

"When a bronc goes to bucking, you got to stand to clear," Noble said to the man who was doubled over. "Let me show you how to hit a man."

Lodero never even saw the punch coming. Noble's fist smashed into the side of his head, and when it did, Lodero's head bounced violently backwards. But the back of his head smashed hard into the nose of the man holding his right arm. The man squealed out, released Lodero's arm and grabbed at his nose that was suddenly pouring blood.

Through the spinning in his brain, Lodero still had the presence of mind to survive.

His arm dropped imperceptibly to his holster, and none of the men saw as his hand clenched the grip of the Peacemaker.

The barrel of the Colt cleared leather and the hammer was cocked in half a second. Lodero drove the barrel of the gun into the stomach of the man holding his left arm, and he pulled the trigger.

The man fell back, shouting in pain and shock, and rolled on the ground.

With no one left to support him, Lodero stumbled and fell to his knees.

But he was still surviving.

He drew his left hand gun, rolled onto his back, and pointed both guns in the direction of where Mullen was still standing below the tree. Lodero thumbed back the hammers of both guns, firing three quick shots that sent Mullen scampering for cover.

Nick Noble didn't wait for Lodero to roll toward him. Nick was already running away.

The man with the broken nose, the one who'd been holding Lodero's right arm, also ran.

His head spinning so that he was hardly aware of what he was doing, Lodero pushed himself from the ground and stumbled back toward the river. The man who was kicked in the groin realized too late that Lodero was coming toward him. The man tried to go for his gun, but Lodero shot him twice, both times in the chest, at very close range. These were surely shots fired to kill. The man wouldn't make it back to town to see the doctor.

Lodero stumbled down the slope of the gulch. He reached the stallion. With his head spinning, he dropped his left hand gun onto the ground and grabbed hold of the pommel. His foot floundered as he leaned against the horse, trying to find the stirrup. A shot rang out behind him and he heard the bullet whiz past. He turned and fired wildly back toward the tree. Mullen was not there, and it had been Nick Noble who had shot anyway.

Lodero's foot slipped into the stirrup, and he gathered what strength he had to step up into the saddle. He slumped forward, dropping his other gun, but Estrellada Nocturno needed no encouragement to run from the danger. More shots rang out as the black stallion bolted out across the river, up the gulch and down the road, back toward the Noble Ranch.

Lodero had no strength to stay in the saddle, but he held tight to the pommel and tried to stay conscious as long as he could.

10

Because the weather had cooled off a bit and it was so pleasant outside, Maria Noble had Juan Carlos Baca and Wash Scotland move a table out to the big porch on the ranch house, and it was there that Maria, the two ranch hands and Wash's family took their supper. They had waited a bit for Lodero, but when he did not appear they decided to eat without him, thinking that he could join them when he arrived. But the food on their plates was diminishing and the shadows were growing longer, and still Lodero did not arrive.

"I should not have let him go alone," Juan Carlos Baca said, breaking the silence at the table.

"I should not have sent him," Maria Noble said.

"He'll be all right," Wash Scotland said. "Boy handles hisself real well." And because he was oblivious to the budding romance on the ranch, he added, "Maybe he's got hisself a girl in town."

Wash's wife, Junie, was not oblivious to the budding

romance between her employer and Lodero, and she subtly nudged Wash under the table with her knee.

Silence again filled the supper table, except for the two children. Wash and Junie had two small children who chatted away freely, unaware of the tension at the table.

Juan Carlos Baca merely picked at his food, his eyes often darting from his plate to the road off in the distance. At last, even as the sun was touching the distant hills to the west, Juan Carlos saw the black horse coming on like a shadow, at first small and distant but then growing in size.

"Eet ees the black without a rider," Juan Carlos announced, standing from the table.

Maria Noble's breath caught in her throat. She stood and saw, too, that the stallion was coming down the road alone.

"I'll get a team hitched to the wagon," Wash Scotland said. He'd seen this before, when he was with the soldiers, a lone and riderless horse returning to its home.

Scotland ran down to the corral and got horses for the wagon. Juan Carlos ran out to the road to meet the black.

Sticky, red wetness on the black's coat and saddle told Juan Carlos that there had been blood. He ran his hands over the horse and found no injuries, and he rightly assumed it was Lodero's blood.

Juan Carlos took the black down to the barn and removed its saddle and tack. He quickly brushed down the stallion and then put him in the corral as Wash was bringing the wagon around. Maria had fetched her guns and saddled a horse. The three of them went down the road, toward town, with Maria riding far out in front of the wagon. Wash had the presence of mind to get some lanterns together because dusk was already upon them.

Maria rode quickly, scanning the ground in the dwindling light. Wash and Juan Carlos went more slowly, methodically searching. Maria was only about two miles south of the ranch when she saw the dark shadow in the middle of the road. Lodero lay where he had fallen from his horse. The wagon was still a ways behind her. She sprang from her saddle and knelt beside Lodero. He was unconscious. Maria ran her hands over him and found a wet patch of blood on his thigh. In the darkness, she moved her fingers over his thigh and discovered both an entry and exit wound. Lodero had been shot through and through. She found no other bullet wounds, but blood on his face told her that he had been beaten as well as shot. She tried to rouse him but could get no response, and she was concerned because his breathing was shallow and labored.

When Wash and Juan Carlos finally arrived with the wagon and lanterns, the extent of Lodero's injuries became obvious. His face was bruised and cut and both eyes were swollen. He had a gash on the back of his head. They tied a handkerchief around the gunshot wound on his leg and another around the gash on his head. Wash and Juan Carlos lifted Lodero onto a blanket, and then they set him as gently as they could into the wagon. Maria tethered her horse to the wagon and rode in the back with Lodero.

Wash Scotland did his best to find the right pace for the wagon -- something between not jostling Lodero too rough and still getting him quickly back to the bunkhouse where they could treat his wounds.

Maria talked to Lodero the entire way, but he was never conscious through the entire journey back to the ranch.

When the wagon at last turned off the road and toward the ranch, Wash directed the horses down toward the bunkhouse.

"Where are you going?" Maria demanded from the back of the wagon.

"Miss Maria, I'm takin' him straight on down to the bunkhouse," Wash said.

"Not to the bunkhouse," Maria said. "My house. Take him to my house."

Wash turned the horses and drove the wagon right up to the front porch of the ranch house. Wash and Juan Carlos, with Maria helping, carried Lodero into the house where they laid him out on the dining table. Maria lit several lanterns. Junie, who was still at the house with the children, gathered up towels and started heating a pot of water.

Maria cleaned the blood from Lodero's face. She cut away his pants to expose the wound on his leg and began cleaning the blood from the wound.

"Best let me take a look," Wash said. "I helped the doctor a few times when I was in the ah-my."

Wash looked at the wound and told Junie to drop some tweezers into boiling water for him. He used the tweezers to dig cloth from Lodero's pants out of the injury.

Juan Carlos Baca became ill and left the room. Maria squeezed Lodero's hand, though he remained unconscious. Junie helped Wash by hold a light where he could better see.

"I'm going to need a bottle of whiskey to pour down

into this so he don't get an infection, and a needle and thread to sew him up. He's lucky this went through the way it did. That lead ball had stayed in his leg, I'd have had to cut him to pieces to get it out. As it is, he'll heal from this before the swelling goes down on them blackened eyes."

While Wash performed the surgery on the kitchen table, Juan Carlos walked out to the corral and looked at Lodero's stallion again. He held a lantern with one hand and ran his other hand all across the horse's side. Satisfied that there was no evidence that the bullet had struck the horse, Juan Carlos walked into the barn and examined Lodero's saddle. There, embedded in the leather of the saddle, he found the lead ball that had struck Lodero's leg.

"Estrellada Nocturno!" Juan Carlos called to the horse. "You were lucky today, mi amigo!"

He thought about Lodero's deep feelings for the horse and felt great relief that when his friend recovered he would still have the black stallion. But Juan Carlos wondered what would happen next. He felt a sudden chill, though the night was not so cold. It seemed to Juan Carlos that he and Lodero were on the precipice, and below them was a raging torrent of violence. Juan Carlos did not doubt that Lodero would leap from the ledge.

After several minutes, Maria Noble was at the back door of the ranch calling to Juan Carlos to come and help move Lodero.

They carried him into Maria's bedroom and put him on her bed. Wash and Juan Carlos undressed him and looked him over for additional injuries. With Maria and Junie both helping, they wrapped his torso because Wash was sure from the bruising that he also had broken ribs. When they were done tending to the injuries, Wash and

Junie took the children and went to their home, and Juan Carlos went down to the bunkhouse.

***

Through the night, Lodero remained unconscious in Maria's bed in the ranch house. Maria stayed up with him, sitting in a high-backed, cushioned chair where she dozed some. She burned lamps through the night so that when she woke she could check on Lodero. She had a pail of water and a cloth, and each time she woke she would squeeze a few drops of water from the cloth into Lodero's mouth.

In the morning, Lodero woke to a soft breeze carrying in the sun through an open window. He hurt all over, and the pain made it impossible for him to move. He was aware of the woman sleeping in the bed beside him, though he could not focus his thoughts enough to even understand who she was. In the early morning hours, exhausted, Maria had left her chair and stretched out in the bed beside Lodero, and there for the first time that night, she slept soundly. Mercifully, Lodero did not stay conscious for more than just a few moments.

When she woke, Maria sent Wash and Juan Carlos to fetch the doctor from town, cautioning them to go directly to the doctor's house and avoid the main street.

Throughout the morning, Lodero dozed fitfully, in and out of sleep and never fully awake or unconscious. In that space between wake and sleep, Lodero began to remember the events from the previous day -- the ambush and the beating, the attempt at hanging him, his lucky escape. He vaguely recalled feeling faint and falling from the saddle. Now he opened his eyes again, feeling more awake but still in extreme discomfort. His entire body ached.

Nothing, except perhaps his toes, did not hurt.

With his eyes open, but still on his back, he only had the smallest view of the room. He knew he did not recognize where he was. But the room had the pretty fragrance of flowers.

Maria rose from the chair and came into Lodero's view, standing over him.

"Miss Maria?" he said, his head groggy and his voice thick.

"Lodero," she said. "You are awake. How do you feel?"

"I feel like I was on the underside of a stampede," Lodero said. "Where are we?"

"Your horse came back to the ranch without you," Maria said. "We found you on the road, beaten and shot."

"Shot?" Lodero asked. He did not remember being shot.

"They shot you in the leg," Maria said. "Washington cleaned the wound and sewed you up last night. A doctor is coming from town."

"Estrellada Nocturno, where is he?"

"In the corral," Maria answered.

"Is he fine?"

"He is fine. He was not hurt."

"And where are we?"

"We are in my bedroom," Maria said. "I did not want to take you to the bunkhouse. It is better for you to be here, in my house, where I can take care of you."

Maria dipped the cloth into the pail of water and held it to Lodero's lips. But he was already exhausted, and he fell back to sleep.

Sleep was mercy because it allowed him to escape the pain.

Later, the doctor from town examined Lodero. He looked at the wounds from the bullet and pronounced Wash Scotland an expert at stitching up gunshot wounds. He decided the gash on Lodero's head should just be bandaged and not sewn shut. He also gave Maria a bottle of laudanum that would allow Lodero to continue to rest while his body healed.

"He's taken a fever, and that concerns me more than the wounds or injuries," the doctor said. "If he can't get over that fever, it could kill him. Give him this meadowsweet elixir to help knock down the fever. Change them bandages and watch for a yellow oozing that might indicate infection. If the wound drains clear and thin, that's fine. But if there is thick, yellow or orange pus, that's bad. Also watch for a redness around the wound to grow. As he is now, I don't see the need for the leg to come off, but if it gets infected I might have to take it. Make up some broth to give him so he can keep up his strength. Nourishment, laudanum, meadowsweet. And if the fever don't break in two days or you see signs of infection, come and get me."

When he woke, Maria put drops of laudanum and drops of the meadowsweet elixir in his water and made him drink. As such, Lodero slept most of the time.

Maria stayed with Lodero constantly to nurse him and to watch for any changes. She had cared for her husband when he took ill, but she had never felt scared like this, even when she knew her husband was dying.

When Lodero was not asleep, the laudanum and the fever combined to make him groggy.

In the evening, while Lodero was asleep, Maria bathed him with a damp cloth.

Even before he was beaten and shot, Maria felt herself drawn to him physically. It had started the moment she saw him. She yearned to be near him. And now, with him asleep in her bed, Maria lied down next to him. She felt the warmth coming from his body. She listened to his labored breathing and put her face close to him so that she could smell his hair. Even though she had bathed him, he smelled like the outdoors to her, he smelled like leather and fresh cut hay. It was a warm and pleasing scent that reminded Maria of summer.

There was a word for what she felt. She was overcome with passion.

Maria had never felt it before -- never as a girl when she worked as a maid in the Noble house, and never as a wife. But now she felt passion, a longing for the stranger who had ridden into her life and risked his own safety by throwing in with her in this fight against the men who were trying to drive her from her ranch.

Perhaps it was more than passion, she thought. Perhaps what she felt was love -- a thing she had heard about, but not the sort of thing a girl who came up the way she did would ever be able to even dream about.

She stayed there beside him, thinking of her childhood and how difficult her life had been. She was raised in poverty, but even when she came out of being poor, she was in a loveless marriage where the unwritten contract with her husband was simply accompaniment and care in his final years.

Late into the night, Lodero stirred. Maria was awake, and in her embarrassment, she jerked herself away from him and off the bed.

"Are you awake?" she asked.

"Were you lying next to me?" Lodero said.

"I was," Maria confessed. And then she offered an explanation. "I am exhausted. I did not sleep much last night."

"I'm takin' up your bed," Lodero said.

"I want you here." She put her hand against his forehead. He was not sweating and no longer felt so hot. "I think your fever has broken."

"You can leave your hand there if you like," Lodero said. "It feels cool, nice."

Maria laughed. She put some drops of laudanum into a glass of water. And even though his fever seemed to have broken, she put some of the meadowsweet elixir in as well.

"I need you to drink this," Maria said.

It was mighty uncomfortable work, but Lodero raised himself up so that he was leaning on an elbow. His head swam with the change of altitude. Maria put the glass to his lips and he drank the little bit of water.

"Tastes foul," he said, lying back down.

"That is the medicine. It is very strong, but you are hurt very bad."

"My head feels like it's about to bust open. Did you tell me earlier that I'd been shot?"

"Through and through, in your thigh," Maria said.

"I suppose that explains why my leg hurts like the dickens. But the hawse is a'right?"

"He is fine. Juan Carlos Baca has made sure. He found the bullet wedged in your saddle."

Maria gently pressed the damp cloth against Lodero's forehead. It was cool and felt nice.

"You have had me very worried," Maria said. "I could not stand it if something happened to you."

Lodero chuckled. "I'd say something did happen to me."

"Something worse," Maria said.

His head was swimming from the laudanum and from the effects of the fever.

"You remind me of a girl from my village," Lodero said dreamily. "Rosita Rios was her name. She was the same age as my sister. Even when I was young, I thought she was the most beautiful girl in the world. Dark, black hair like you. Brown eyes, a light, pretty brown like your eyes. Soft eyes. Smoky eyes. You make me think of her. Even when we first came to the ranch, I said to Juan Carlos that you make me think of her."

He was rambling in his delirium.

"Rosita Rios. Her father died and she left our village to be with family. She was a Tejano. Juan Carlos said she moved to Old Mexico. It broke my heart when she left. I was young, but I believe I loved her."

"Rosita Maria Rios," Maria said, taking up Lodero's story. "She did not move to Old Mexico. She moved to San

Antone. Her family was very poor in the village where she grew up, and when her father died they had to go where they could find work. Her mother became a cook at a hotel, and Rosita became a maid for a wealthy couple. The woman died, but the old man, he wanted a companion in his old age. And he liked the maid. But he told Rosita to go by her middle name, Maria, and he married her and built a ranch far away from San Antone where he would not have to feel the shame from his wealthy friends for marrying a Tejano."

Lodero looked into Maria's eyes, he was slow to catch on because the laudanum was clouding his mind.

"What are you saying?" he asked.

Maria leaned forward so that she was very close to Lodero's ear, and she whispered a name to him.

"That name? How do you know that name if you are not Rosita?" Lodero asked.

"I know that name because I am Rosita," she said. "Rosita Maria Rios Noble. It is a big name for the little girl you knew in your village, Lodero. And I know you, though I would have never recognized you. But I did recognize Juan Carlos Baca, and I knew your sister and was friends with her."

Maria gently pressed her lips against Lodero's lips. Her lips were soft and tasted like vanilla.

"You are not the little boy from the village any longer," Maria whispered. "May I lie back down beside you?"

Lodero could not keep his eyes open. His brain was fogged over.

"Lie with me, Rosita," he whispered. And she did.

11

It was not until three days later that Lodero was awake and aware enough to tell his story, and Juan Carlos and Wash were both present with Maria to hear it. Wash had made up a crutch and the two men brought it up to the house so that Lodero could give it a try.

They had to gingerly help him from the bed because his bruised rips were still tender, and both Wash and Juan Carlos stood nearby because Lodero's head reeled each time he moved about. But they stood him from the side of the bed and put the crutch under his arm, and though it was exhausting and difficult, Lodero was able to lean against the crutch and walk the length of the room and down the hall and back.

His fever was gone, and he only took the laudanum now to help him sleep at night.

After trying his crutch, Lodero laid back into the bed in Maria's room and gave an account to Wash and Juan Carlos of what had happened on his ride back from town. He told them how he had seen Mullen in town and had a bad feeling as he rode back to the ranch. He told them how he had been bushwhacked there at the river.

"I never saw them come up on me. I think they must have been hiding and waiting for me. I never saw any sign of their horses, either, so they must have been there for some time."

He told them about Nick Noble's warning -- the gist of what he could remember -- and Mullen and Noble standing below the cottonwood tree with a rope thrown over a branch.

"Do you think they intended to hang you?" Maria asked.

"I am sure of it," Lodero said.

"You must be extra vigilant of the stock now," Lodero said to Wash and Juan Carlos. "They'll know I'm hurt and that I ain't no use around here right now. If they want to drive off the cattle, now is the best time for them to do it."

"We brought them in from the far pastures," Wash said. "Ain't as much good grazing grass this close to the ranch, but it's easier to keep an eye on the stock. I'll sure rest easier when you're back out there with us."

Juan Carlos Baca stood in a corner of the room. He had not said much, if anything, and had only looked at Lodero with a worried expression.

"Juan Carlos, why do you look so upset?"

Juan Carlos looked first to Wash and then to Maria Noble. "Could I speak privately with Lodero?" he asked.

Wash Scotland didn't like it. Since they'd found Lodero, the old Mexican had become less talkative and less friendly. Scotland knew he needed the two men to help at the ranch -- if not them, then someone. He was afraid that Juan Carlos was ready to make tracks.

Maria Noble, though she shared Scotland's concerns, immediately walked to the door of her bedroom. "Certainly, Juan Carlos. Mr. Scotland, why don't we go see if Mrs. Scotland needs a hand with supper."

Maria closed the bedroom door behind them.

"What is it, Juan Carlos?" Lodero asked.

Juan Carlos did not hesitate. He'd been working on this speech for three days.

"As soon as you are fit to ride, we should leave this place," he said. "Eet ees too dangerous here. These men are no normal cattle rustlers. They are killers, and you are lucky to still be alive. We set out on this journey together for a reason, and we have now abandoned that reason to become cowpunchers. You and I, mi amigo, we should return to our purpose. We should start for El Paso immediately. And then on to Silver City, if we think that is where our journey will lead."

Still, three days later, Lodero's head throbbed with pain and he found it difficult to think. He did not want to argue with Juan Carlos. "I made the Noble widow a promise," he said. "We will see that her cattle make it to the spring drive."

Juan Carlos sighed heavily. "We do not need to buy trouble," he said. "Those men tried to hang you from a tree, and this is not our fight. These are not our cattle. This is not our ranch. And this is not our fight."

"Maria is Rosita Rios from our village, Juan Carlos."

"She told you that?" Juan Carlos asked.

"She did."

"Eet changes nothing. We should not stay here."

"You're right, Juan Carlos. It changes nothing. I would stay even if she was not Rosita Rios."

Lodero shifted himself in the bed and winced at the pain that shot like an echo through his leg and through his head, intense and lingering. He was exhausted from the effort of walking with the crutch.

"My old friend, you know as well as I do that I cannot leave here. Whether this is our fight or not, we've stumbled into it. What these men -- Nick Noble and the lawyer -- what they are trying to do is wrong. And I do not think you are the kind of man who sees a woman gettin' bulldozed like this and walks away from her to fend for herself. I know I ain't that kind of man. Now I won't go back on the promise I made to the widow. And I don't think you will either. But you ain't bound by my promise, and it was my promise, so if you want to go, then I ain't goin' to stop you."

Juan Carlos hemmed and hawed over it. He started to speak and stopped himself. Then he did it again. He paced back and forth at the foot of the bed, breathing heavily and moving his hands about as if he was having an internal conversation. At last he said, "Eet ees not me I worry over. Those men almost hanged you. I do not want to see you die over this widow's fight. I suspect you have taken a liking to her, and so maybe eet ees becoming your fight. But what about the empty trunk? What about El Paso and Silver City?"

"I'm still bound to find where that empty trunk

106

came from, and who emptied it," Lodero said. "I'm still goin' to El Paso, and Silver City. But I ain't leavin' here until them cattle are on the drive."

"And you believe her, you are sure, that she is Rosita Rios from our village?"

"I am sure," Lodero said. "When we spoke of it, she told me my father's name."

"She knows your father's name?" Juan Carlos said, suddenly surprised. "She used it? She called you by your father's name?"

"She did."

"Oh, this is worse," Juan Carlos said. "You must make her swear to never say that name again."

"I will make her swear," Lodero said. "Do not worry over that, Juan Carlos."

Juan Carlos Baca stood silently for a long time, looking out the window. "Of course, I will stay if you stay. But when the stock is gone and Rosita Maria, the Noble widow, is paid for her cattle, we will go on. Yes?"

"Yes."

"Swear eet to me, as you made a promise to the Noble widow, make a promise to your old amigo."

"I promise, Juan Carlos Baca."

"Even if you come back here," Juan Carlos Baca said. "If you come back here and I go home to our village alone, you promise me we will go and find where the empty trunk came from."

"If I come back here, Juan Carlos, you will come back with me. I am too accustomed to having you around."

Juan Carlos left the bedroom door opened behind him and went back out to the bunkhouse.

The widow Noble returned to her bedroom.

"Juan Carlos does not seem happy," she said. "I will guess at the cause of his mood. He wants to leave because he believes Nick Noble and Brad Decker will come after you again. He thinks it is unsafe for you. And you are refusing to go."

Lodero grinned at her. "You have guessed so well that I would be justified to accuse you of listening at the door."

"I did not listen at the door, but I share his worries. I have been thinking about it. Maybe I should try to sell the ranch."

"You love this ranch," Lodero said. "Why would you sell it?"

"I could get the money I need to pay off the loan at the bank, and there would be more there. Money that I could go someplace and start over."

"You will not sell this ranch," Lodero said. "We will protect your cattle until the spring drive and you can get paid. And that is where you will get the money to pay off the loan."

"But what if they come after you again? What if the second time they are successful and they kill you?"

Lodero clenched his teeth. "They will not catch me unprepared for them again. I promise you that. Selling the ranch is not the answer."

Maria persisted. "What if I said that we could go somewhere, together? I could sell the ranch, pay the loan from the bank, and with the money left, we could go together."

"When the stock is gone on the spring drive, Juan Carlos and I have a job to finish."

"What job?" Maria asked.

"We still have to go to El Paso, and then to Silver City."

"What is there?" Maria asked. "What is in El Paso and Silver City?"

This was not a story Lodero had told before. There were few who knew it -- Juan Carlos Baca knew the story because he had been there. But Lodero had never told the story to another person.

"When I was a boy, my father was my hero," Lodero said. "He seemed so large to me. He was everything a man should be, tough and strong and brave. But he was also loving to me and my sister, and I remember his easy way with my mother and how she always smiled when he wrapped her in his arms. And there was always Juan Carlos Baca telling stories of the old days, how my father fought bravely against the Mexicans. He seemed like the hero from a dime novel, and yet he was my father."

Lodero paused as he thought about the days spent with his father when he was just a boy.

"He taught me how to ride and how to shoot. He taught me how to handle hawses and how to treat women with kindness and care and respect. He taught me how to be a decent man. And he lived the example. We were not wealthy, but we got by.

"One morning, my father hitched a wagon to a

couple of mules, tied his hawse to the back, and he left our home to go off and seek his fortune. He left me and my mother and my sister. I guess this was just after the War of Secession when he left, and I'd have been about ten or eleven years old. He said he could not stand any longer to eke out an existence in that barren village where we lived, and he was determined to find some way to make a better life. When he found that better life, he said, he would come back for us.

"I reckon it was a year, but it might have been two, after he left, we received a letter from him that he wrote from El Paso. In the letter he said that he had found men who were going into Arizona Territory to mine for gold and silver and that he was going to go with them. In that letter, he said he had left something for the family in El Paso, and if something happened and he never came home, we should go there and get it. That was the last we heard from him.

"My mother always said he must have been killed. My father loved my mother very much, and she believed that the only thing that would have kept him from coming back for her was if he was dead.

"A few years later, his trunk was delivered to our home. When we opened it, the trunk -- my father's trunk -- was empty. Pinned to the lining inside was a note that said the sender was returning the trunk at my father's request. The note was signed only with the initials 'R.G.'

"The trunk was shipped to us from Silver City, New Mexico Territory. The lock had been tampered. We believe there was something in the trunk when it was shipped to us, and that someone stole whatever was inside.

"My mother took the empty trunk as confirmation that my father was dead. The proof that dashed the flicker of hope she'd held to for so long. She was heartbroken, and she died of a broken heart not long after we received the empty trunk. And when she died, I stood over her grave and I made a promise to my mother that I would find what had happened to my father. And Juan Carlos, who rode with my father in the War with Mexico, he promised he would come with me.

"And so we are going on to El Paso in the hopes of finding out who my father went to the New Mexico Territory with, and then we are going to Silver City to find the man with the initials R.G., and to discover what became of my father."

Maria sat quietly after Lodero had finished his tale.

"And you never went to El Paso to see what your father had left for you there?"

"My mother never wanted to go. My sister and me, we both tried to get her to. But she said that part of her life that she spent with my father was done, and she would just go on in our village and El Paso could keep whatever it was my father left there."

"I am so sorry for your mother."

"I was sorry, too. She was mighty sad at the end of her life. And it was hard to bury her knowing that she never had any answer of what happened to the man she loved. It pains me to think of it, and I have hope that they are together now, reunited in the life after this one.

"So Juan Carlos and I will get your cattle on the spring drive. You can get the money to pay back the bank. But then we will have to go. We have business in El Paso and Silver City."

Lodero could feel the intensity of Maria's dark eyes

as she watched him talk. She never took her eyes off of him.

"And after Silver City?" Maria asked. "You said once that you would come back here if I asked you to."

"If you asked me to, I reckon I would."

Maria said nothing more. She made no request, nor did she elicit a promise. But what she knew was that if she made the request and received the promise, nothing would prevent Lodero from coming back.

***

Lodero spent a week with the crutch in his armpit, able only to get around near the ranch house. Then he transitioned from crutch to cane and was able to limp farther out, all the way down to the bunkhouse. When he was able to get from the house to the bunkhouse on the cane, he surrendered Maria's bed back to her and moved back into the bunkhouse with Juan Carlos.

No one at the ranch talked, but Lodero worried that the longer he stayed in the ranch house the more likely word would get out that he was living in the house. He did not want to be the cause of rumors that would sully Maria Noble's reputation. He didn't know, either, if his presence in the ranch house might be used by the lawyer Brad Decker to bring some sort of lawsuit against Maria, challenging her right to the inheritance of her husband's ranch. These things happened, he knew.

Though deep feelings were growing between them, those rumors would have been unfounded. Lodero's presence in Maria's bed had been without guilt or sin, unless talk was sin. He wanted her desperately, and he believed she wanted him, but Lodero refused to do a thing from selfish desire that might risk her future.

The winter days were not particularly harsh that year, though the nights were cold. As his leg healed, Lodero spent many days chopping wood for the ranch house and bunkhouse stoves to keep them warm through the nights. Juan Carlos, proud that he had become a real vaquero, helped Wash Scotland keep the stock near the ranch house, and Lodero limited his riding to short forays across the ranch looking for signs of rustlers or intruders on the property. He was pleased to be able to return to the saddle. The stallion was like an old friend to him, and those days he spent on the crutch and cane with his head and leg too sore for riding, had been lonely days away from his friend. Estrellada Nocturno, too, seemed to relish the rides, short as they were.

On the coldest day of the winter, with just a smattering of snow sticking to the ground, Wash and Lodero rode out across the ranch to look for strays and push the cattle to a fresh grazing pasture. They had tied scarves across their faces because the wind was brutal, and the white flakes in the air seemed to have a knack for getting under their hat brims to land and freeze on all the exposed places.

After bringing in a few strays, Wash dismounted and started up a fire for warmth and coffee. Lodero collected up wood so that after the coffee was brewed they could pile on a few good sized branches to get a warm fire going.

"They's a war coming, sho 'nuff," Wash said, holding his tin cup in both hands and letting the heat come through his gloves.

"You reckon?"

"I do. That boy Nick Noble, he's determined to get

PEECHER

this 'ere ranch, and he knows the way to do it is to drive off the stock. Miss Maria can't hold out another year if she misses the spring cattle drive. Time is running out. It's cold today, but we ain't but a couple of months from the cattle drive, now. So I ask myself, if he's determined to drive off the cattle, what's this Lodero fellow determined to do?"

Wash tilted his head toward Lodero to give him the opportunity to answer the question.

"I promised Miss Noble I'd see her cattle make it to the drive," Lodero said. "That's what I'm bound to do."

"Yep," Wash said. "Old Abe Lincoln said he was determined to keep them states together. And Jeff Davis said he was determined to get 'em separate. What happens any time you got two men determined on incongruous tracks?"

Lodero didn't see much point in argument. Wash was probably right. Unless Nick Noble backed down, Lodero figured there was probably going to be killing.

"Does it make you nervous, knowin' men is going to get killed over a piece of land?"

"Men have been killed over a piece of land before," Lodero said.

"What if it's you?"

"I don't reckon it will be. Them men bushwhacked me once. I won't let that happen again. I figure in a fair fight, none of them stand much chance."

"That's big talk," Wash said. "You sho you can back that up?"

"Mighty close to sure," Lodero said.

"Mullen? He's a quick gun is what they say," Wash said. "He's just a cowpuncher, all he's ever been. He used to work out here on the ranch. I knew Jake Mullen well, and I'm disappointed in him. But he wants to be a gunman, and he practiced all the time when he was working here on the ranch. Spinning guns, drawin' and shootin'. I've seen him draw mighty quick."

Lodero shrugged and stepped closer to the fire so that the heat would come up against his trousers and warm his legs. The smoke blew into his face, but he ignored it.

"Lots of folks is quick. Sometimes quick ain't what matters. Bein' able to hit what you're shooting at matters a whole lot more than bein' quick. What else can you tell me about Mullen?"

"He was in the cavalry, like me," Wash said. "I never knew him. You could probably guess by looking that he warn't in the colored units." Wash laughed at his own joke. "He was at a fawt up in Kansas or Nebraska or someplace. I don't recollect. But we got along all right on account of both of us bein' from the cavalry."

Wash fell silent and thoughtful, and sipped on his coffee for a bit without making more conversation. The whole time, though, his eyes were looking over the rim of the tin cup at Lodero.

"I done my bit against the Injuns," Wash said. "We had some tough scrapes with them old boys, and I fought 'em pretty hard. Killed a fair few of 'em and got shot at more than I cared for. Fightin' Injuns is frightening business. They love to get you when they got numbers on you. They love to sneak up on you. And what they do to a man they catch is beyond cruelty. But I never run from 'em. I always did my bit."

Lodero had no response. He'd heard of the Indian fights and heard of the way the Comanche and Apache could desecrate a body. He didn't doubt that it was frightening. He was glad to have never encountered a band of warriors off the reservation and hoped that he never would.

"The thing is, Lodero, I done my bit before I had a wife and them young'uns. It ain't fair to them, now, for me to go off and get myself killed."

"I understand that, Wash," Lodero said. "A man's got to take care of his own."

"It ain't fear, you understand. I ain't afeared of no man. But I got a family countin' on me. And when this thing comes to war, you've got to count me out. I'll do what I can to keep these cattle critters on the ranch, and I'll work 'em like they was my own. But when men go to throwin' guns, Ol' Wash Scotland ain't gonna be counted among 'em."

Lodero walked away from the fire and looked out across the cattle, all standing pretty near each other with the cold wind blowing. He didn't much care for the cold. In his village, down by the border, cold weather like this never came. Snow was an unknown thing, and temperatures seldom dropped much below fifty degrees. He was eager to get back to the bunkhouse. He walked back over to the fire, and his leg was stiff in the cold weather.

"Wash, ain't nobody going to think less of you for taking care of your own. I appreciate you lettin' me know where you stand. All I would ask is if they get to me, you do what you can for Miss Noble."

12

At the time that the first golden green leaves broke out on the mesquite and the sage purpled over with the early rains of spring, Maria Noble, Wash and his family, Lodero, and Juan Carlos were all sitting at the table on the porch having Sunday supper when a man on horseback turned off the road and came toward the ranch. Maria walked out toward the road to greet the man on horseback, and she spent several minutes talking to him.

"That thar's Jimmy Cook," Wash explained. "He's from a ranch south of town, and he's the trail boss that will take Miss Maria's cattle. I sho hope his showin' up here today don't tell of bad tidings."

"Why would it?" Lodero asked.

"If Nick Noble has got to him, or that lawyer Decker, and convinced him not to take Miss Maria's critters."

Lodero watched the conversation between Cook, who did not leave his saddle, and the Noble widow, trying to judge from her body language if there was bad news.

"Ol' Jimmy Cook ain't one to scare off of a job, but he might be bought. But he runs a big crew, a dozen men or more, and they only make money if he's got enough head o' critters. He has to pull stock off of three or four ranches to make his money. That works to our favor. Mr. Cook has got his own ranch, but a small herd. He always drove the cattle for Mr. Noble, and I think he's a loyal man. That works to our favor, too.

At length the interview between Maria Noble and Jimmy Cook concluded, and the man rode back toward the south, the way he'd come.

"Ain't stayin' for supper," Wash commented. "That don't seem to work in our favor."

Lodero could gather nothing from Maria's stride as she returned to the table. She slid out her own chair and sat back down at the table.

"Three weeks," she announced. "Mr. Cook says he'll start the cattle north on the main road, and bring our herd into the group when they get here. He plans to drive the cattle from the other ranches here and spend a night. The next day he wants to give all of our herd the road brand. And he wants to be started for Kansas the next day. We'll need to cut out those that are not going and bring the others in so that we can make quick work of the road branding. Mr. Cook has heard the rumors of our troubles, and he has no interest in lingering here longer than necessary."

"Strange that we've seen nothing of Nick Noble and his men all winter," Lodero said. "We might expect trouble before three weeks have expired."

"We might indeed," Maria said. "Mr. Cook seems to think we should expect trouble. He said the rumor in town is that three strangers have shown up at the hotel and been seen dining with that man Mullen, Nick, and Bradford Decker."

"And what does eet mean?" Juan Carlos asked. "Who are these three men?"

Maria kept her eyes on her plate as she answered. "Mr. Cook seems to think these are men who are hired only for their skill with a gun."

Suddenly she dropped her fork down onto the plate and stood up, turning away from the table. She started toward the house, leaving the others at the table bewildered. But she stopped at the door and, without turning around, the Noble widow said, "Lodero, will you come and speak to me?"

Lodero glanced at Wash and Juan Carlos Baca, both of whom gave him curious looks.

"Yes ma'am," Lodero said, rising from the table to follow Maria into the house. Juan Carlos Baca watched him go, and it occurred to Juan Carlos that if there was still a limp, it was imperceptible. Lodero's stride was back to the tall, confident stride he'd had before the shooting.

When he got inside, he found her with her face in her hands.

"What is it?" Lodero asked, his voice full of concern.

Maria moved her hands to look at him, and he saw that she was in tears.

"Oh, Lodero!" she exclaimed, and threw herself into his arms. "I do not know if I can do it. I do not know if I can go through with this!"

"What is it, Maria?" Lodero asked, wrapping his

119

arms around her and holding her against him. "Your courage can't fail now. We're three weeks from the cattle drive. We've nearly made it."

"Jimmy Cook told me that Brad Decker has hired real gunmen. These three men who came to town, they're bad men -- killers. They're not like Mullen. He's just a local cowpuncher pretending to be a tough man who intimidates folks for a living. But these are real gun fighters.

"And they're here to kill you," Maria said.

"We knew something like this could happen," Lodero said. "I ain't scared."

"I could sell the ranch," Maria said. "I could sell it to Jimmy Cook. He'd pay a decent price for it. There's others, too, who would buy it from me, and Nick would not get it."

"Is that what you want?" Lodero asked.

Maria was quiet in his arms for a moment. She had stopped crying.

"No," she said. "I do not want to sell the ranch. I want to keep it, grow it, make it into something."

"Then I reckon we won't talk any more of selling the ranch," Lodero said. "We have to get through three weeks. We'll keep a constant watch on the stock to make certain Nick and his men don't ride in and rustle your cattle."

"I don't want anything to happen to you or Juan Carlos," Maria said. "How could I live with it if something terrible happened -- if one of you was killed -- and it was in the name of protecting my herd?"

"You ain't got to worry about that, Miss Maria," Lodero said. "Juan Carlos Baca can handle himself pretty well, and I reckon I can, too."

Lodero reached up to his neck and slid loose the kerchief he had tied there. He unrolled it and slapped it once against his leg, to beat off any dust that might be there. Then he used it to wipe the tears away from Maria's face.

"I guess I can't stand to see a woman cry," he said. "I don't want you to worry over this. We'll do what we have to do to get your cattle on the drive. My question, though, how do you know Nick won't go after your cattle when they're on the trail?"

Maria shook her head. "He would not try such a thing. There are three other ranchers who are sending their cattle north with Jimmy Cook. Even if Nick could rustle cattle away from Jimmy -- and I don't think he can -- he would not dare to threaten the stock of other ranchers. They would kill him if he did such a thing."

Lodero found himself tempted to ride into town and find Mullen and fight this out now. But an aggressive move like that would probably be viewed as murder. Anything Lodero did, he was going to have to let Noble and his men come at him if he wanted to avoid a murder charge.

"Three weeks is not so long for us to be brave," Lodero said. "We can be strong for three weeks, and then there can be an end to all of this."

Maria nodded, her face red with emotion. She reached a hand up and touched it against Lodero's cheek.

"I know you're right," she said. "I cannot give in or back down. But when I think of how you suffered when you were beaten and shot, and knowing that more violence lies across our path if we keep moving forward, it is hard to be strong and brave."

"It's hard, sure," Lodero agreed. "But I reckon there is no other choice. You want to keep this ranch, and I made you a promise. If you sold it now, I would be forced to break my word to you."

Maria bit her lower lip and nodded agreement with her eyes shut. "I know you are right. I know our course is determined for us. But I am scared."

"Let's go and finish our supper. Tonight I'll ride out to the pasture and keep a watch until sunup. Then you come out and relieve me. We'll take it in shifts."

13

Lodero rode far out on the ranch, beyond the pastures where the cattle were grazing. The best water on the ranch, and the best grazing pastures, were out to the west near the edge of Maria Noble's property. It was out here where Nick Noble's men had caused a stampede and where Lodero had first encountered Mullen. He was looking for sign that anyone had trespassed on the ranch out here.

The rumor Jimmy Cook brought to the Noble Ranch on Sunday was that Nick Noble and Brad Decker had hired gunmen, real gunslingers who would come here to do murder. If it was true, these were not likely to be men who would stand up in a fair fight. Lodero calculated that Jake Mullen probably wouldn't backshoot him. But these men almost surely would. His fear was that they would set up somewhere on the ranch with a rifle and wait for their moment. They would kill from a distance. With Lodero dead, it would be an easy thing to drive the cattle off the ranch. All that would stand in their way was a slow, fat, old Tejano, a Buffalo Soldier who was finished with fighting, and a woman.

So Lodero rode out across the pastures, creeks, and broken country of the ranch, looking for any sign that these hired gunmen had been trespassing on the Noble Ranch.

Late in the afternoon, having satisfied himself that the western reaches of the ranch had not been invaded, Lodero turned the black back toward the ranch house.

The ride was pleasant. The early spring was still not so hot, and Estrellada Nocturno enjoyed the run. Lodero's head no longer throbbed when he was mounted on his horse, and his leg no longer stiffened up on him. For the first time in many weeks, he felt particularly good, and the stallion seemed to sense it. But when he arrived back at the bunkhouse, all his good feelings evaporated. Even from a distance, Lodero could see Juan Carlos Baca outside of the bunkhouse, a double-barrel scatter gun in his hands, and three men were seated on the ground -- all three of them sitting on their own hands.

As Lodero neared, he could see that one of the men on the ground was Jake Mullen, held under the threat of Juan Carlos's scatter gun.

The stallion wanted to head to the corral and fresh hay, but Lodero directed him to the bunkhouse, and once he was there he leapt from the saddle.

"What's happening here?" he asked, walking to Juan Carlos, who did not take his eyes off the three men.

"I do not know what to think of this," Juan Carlos said. "So I have held these men until your return."

Jake Mullen started to get up, but Juan Carlos swung the barrels of the shotgun on him. "You sit on your hands until we tell you to stand."

All three men were wearing empty holsters. Lodero

noticed four guns sitting on a table outside the bunkhouse. He recognized two of the guns as being Mullen's. The other two men only wore a single holster apiece.

"They rode into the ranch about an hour ago," Juan Carlos said. "They said something bad has happened in town, and they want to talk to you. So I said to them to set their guns on the table and sit on their hands. They have been like this for an hour now."

"I reckon if you've got something to say, you'd best get it said," Lodero said, looking at Mullen.

Mullen cleared his throat. He was clearly nervous with the scatter gun pointed at him.

"First thing I want to say is that I didn't have anything to do with this," Mullen said.

Even as Jake Mullen spoke, Lodero scanned the farm. He noticed right away that the wagon and a couple of the draft horses were missing.

"Where is Maria?" Lodero asked.

"She and Washington went into town for supplies," Juan Carlos said. "They went after you left this morning."

Lodero was overcome with a sense of dread. "What has happened?" he asked Mullen.

"Miss Noble and Wash Scotland come to the supply store in town earlier today," Mullen said. "Noble and Decker, they hired some gunmen -- killers -- to come here and deal with you. But they were in town today, like they have been. They figured with the coming of spring you'd be in town eventually for supplies. Their thought was to bushwhack you on your way to the farm, like we did back in the fall."

"I remember," Lodero said.

Mullen frowned. "I feel real bad about that."

"What happened in town?"

"So these hired men, they saw Scotland and Miss Noble. I guess it was Nick that pointed them out. So they walked over to the store and started in on Wash Scotland. Started calling him names, you know what I mean. They were taunting him, trying to provoke him. But Wash wouldn't be provoked. Nothing they said raised his ire. Then the next thing I know, one of them throws his gun and fires three shots into Wash. Killed him dead right there in the middle of town."

"They killed Wash?" Lodero repeated.

"It was murder," Jake Mullen said. "You know I worked with him here on the ranch. I never wanted no harm to come to Washington. He was a good and a decent man."

Lodero's fury boiled over. He reached down and grabbed Mullen by the front of his shirt and dragged him to his feet. "What do you mean they killed Wash?" Lodero demanded, his face contorted in a rage.

Mullen made no effort to fight back or defend himself. He put his arms out to the sides, palms up. "I had nothing to do with it," Mullen said. "I ain't a part of what happened."

Lodero held tight to the wads of Mullen's shirt. "Are you saying they just shot and killed him for no reason?"

"That's what happened."

"And what about the law? The sheriff?"

"The sheriff's after them. He was putting together a posse when I left town to come out here."

"They ran?"

"Sure," Mullen said. "They gunned down a man in the middle of the street for no reason. Plenty of witnesses. They ran."

"What about Maria?" Lodero asked.

"Well that's what I come out here for," Mullen said. "I come out to tell you, they took her."

Lodero's heart thumped heavy in his chest. He shook Mullen. "Took her? Took her where?"

"Let go of me and listen to me," Mullen said. "I'm here to help you."

Lodero's instinct was to swing his fists, but he turned loose of Mullen's shirt.

Mullen breathed heavy and looked at the dirt, forming his thoughts. He nodded to himself and then looked Lodero square in the eye.

"I didn't want what happened to Wash," Mullen said. "That ain't what I signed up for. Truth is, I don't know what I signed up for. It went from rustling cattle to something more awful fast, and I guess I just got swept up in it. Them men that come to town last week, they's bad men, and Nick Noble knew what he was hiring with them. When they saw Wash and Miss Noble come to town, they come up with a plan to taunt Wash to draw on them. I knew he wouldn't, so I went along. I knew there wasn't nothing they could say that would provoke Wash to pull his iron. But when they couldn't get him to jump, one of them men just throwed his gun and shot Wash dead.

"Then everything happened fast. Them men jumped on their hawses, and one of them snatched up Miss Noble, and they rode out fast. Nick rode out with them. Folks went to get the sheriff, and he said he was going after them. But I come out here to fetch you. I don't reckon the sheriff is going to find them."

"Why is that?" Lodero asked.

"The sheriff ain't a bad man, but he don't know how to track. He ain't got anybody in the posse that can track, neither."

"But you can track?" Lodero asked.

"I don't have to track," Mullen said. "Anyhow, I know right where they went."

"So why tell me? Why not go to the sheriff and tell him where they've gone?" Lodero asked.

Mullen shrugged. "If I tell the sheriff and the posse how to find Noble and them others, they might go and arrest 'em. And come time for a trial, maybe they weasel out of it. Maybe only the one that pulled the trigger gets hung. Maybe there ain't no justice for none of them. Wash Scotland deserves justice, and I reckon you're a better man than the sheriff, anyhow, to get Wash the kind of justice he deserves."

"Tell me where they've gone," Lodero said.

"I come out here to throw in with you," Mullen said. "I'll take you to them. You'll need help, anyhow."

"What about these boys?" Lodero asked, looking at the men sitting on the ground.

"This is Blake Alsworth and Sam Lawrence," Mullen said, and the men tipped their heads to Lodero. "They worked out here at one time, too. Both of 'em knew Wash. I figured somebody had to look after the stock if you and me was going after Miss Noble. So they's come out here to watch the cattle."

Lodero cast a glance to Juan Carlos, who was still holding the scatter gun in menacing fashion. If Mullen's story was true, they needed to move on now. But it could just as easily be a trap of some kind to lure Lodero from the ranch to make it easy on Alsworth and Lawrence to drive off Maria's cattle.

"How do I know you're being truthful?" Lodero asked.

"You don't," Mullen conceded. "All I can offer you is my word."

The man sitting on his hands who Mullen had identified as Blake Alsworth spoke up, "Everything he's saying is true, mister."

In a rough country where men sometimes were forced to depend on others for help, a man's word was all he had. Most men took that serious, and their word was more important to them than just about anything else. Others considered themselves free from the promises they made. A trusting man could be lured astray easy, and so just as a man had to be honest and keep his word, so too did men have to be judicious in their ability to know which men could be trusted.

There was something about Mullen that Lodero thought he could trust, though the last time they'd seen each other, Mullen had stood with noose in hand intending to hang Lodero.

"Saddle your hawse," Lodero said to Juan Carlos. "If

this man backshoots me, you be ready to kill him. If he's telling the truth, we'll need your help."

Relief filled Jake Mullen's face. "I thank you for believing me," he said.

"I don't yet know if I believe you," Lodero said. "But I believe you enough to give you the opportunity to shoot me in the back if that's what you're intending."

14

"Spare your hawses," Jake Mullen told Lodero and Juan Carlos. "We got time because they won't hurt the Miss Noble. But depending on how all this falls out, we may need these hawses to be fit to run later." To Lodero he added, "You're the one they want, anyhow."

Lodero and Mullen rode side by side at an easy pace where they could talk. By choice, Juan Carlos Baca rode behind them and kept his scatter gun resting across the front of his saddle. He did not trust Mullen, and though he'd kept his misgivings to himself, he worried that Mullen's intention was to lead them to a trap.

"Then why did they go after Wash?" Lodero asked.

"They thought they could rile him and get him to draw," Mullen said. "They planned it like that so they could shoot him and call it self-defense. They figured if they shot Wash in town, you'd ride in for vengeance. And then they figured they could shoot you and call it self-defense, again. With you and Wash both dead, their plan was to run off the cattle in the next few days, well ahead of the spring drive.

But they didn't figure on Wash being the kind of man who couldn't be riled, being unwilling to throw his gun. And when they shot him anyhow, in front of them witnesses, they couldn't claim that was self-defense. It was murder, and everyone knew it."

Lodero shook his head in dismay. Over a piece of land, they'd gunned down a good man. "Wash told me he would stay out of it if it came to guns."

"He tried, anyhow," Mullen said. "It didn't matter what them men said or did, Wash Scotland wouldn't be provoked."

"What will they do now?" Lodero asked.

"They've gone to hide out, probably figure out what their next play is going to be. They fouled it up. Nick Noble was cussing them fierce when they shot Wash the way they did. Miss Noble, she ran over to Wash, but I could see from where I was that he was dead when he hit the ground. All of them panicked -- them three gunfighters Noble hired -- and they went for their hawses. As he was riding past, the one that calls hisself the Valdosta Kid, he snatched Miss Noble up off the ground, held her on his hawse, and he galloped on away behind the others."

"'The Valdosta Kid'?" Lodero asked. "What the hell kind of name is that?"

"It's what he goes by. He's a fast draw man. Brags a good bit that he's killed seven men," Mullen said.

"Is it true? Has he killed seven men?"

"It's what he brags about, anyhow," Mullen said.

"So they've got The Valdosta Kid with them, a fast gun who's killed seven men," Lodero said. "Who else?"

"Valdosta, he's just a kid, not but maybe twenty years old. He talks a lot, mostly about how fast he is with the gun. He's the one that shot Wash. Then there's Tom Massey. He's sort of the leader of the three. He's an older fellow, I would guess he's in his forties. Real steady. Doesn't talk much, but he handles all the deals. Nick Noble talks to Tom Massey, and Massey talks to the other two."

"What about the third one?" Lodero asked.

"He's young, like the Valdosta Kid. But he's not as mouthy. His name is Danny Walker. Carries a couple of pearl handle Colts. He's always got one in his hand, twirling it. He ain't showing off. He's just keeping it in his hand, feeling the weight of it."

"How many men has Danny Walker killed?" Lodero asked.

"He never said," Jake Mullen admitted.

Lodero thought through the brief descriptions. In his mind, he wanted to think through the scenario of what it would look like when he had to throw guns with these men.

"What else can you tell me?"

"Massey was a buffalo runner. He carries a big Sharps rifle in a scabbard on his hawse. He wanted to set up on the ranch and shoot you from a distance. Bushwhack you so that you never had a chance. But Nick Noble opposed that plan. Noble wanted something that wouldn't seem like murder. Nick wants that ranch, but he doesn't want it to be tainted. He doesn't want everyone in the county thinking he committed murder to get the ranch. That's why they wanted to set up Wash. They figured if they killed him, it would draw you out."

"So it was Nick Noble's plan to start this by killing

Wash?" Lodero asked.

"It was," Mullen said.

Nick Noble would have to die. Lodero was riding to get Maria back safely, but he was also planning vengeance. Lodero was not the man who would allow a cold-blooded murder to stand without answer. If Nick Noble plotted this, Lodero intended to kill Nick Noble.

The other three -- Massey the buffalo runner, the mouthy Kid Valdosta, and Danny Walker who twirls his gun -- they would have to die, too.

"Which one shot Wash?" Lodero asked.

"Valdosta," Mullen said. "When it was obvious Wash wasn't going to throw guns with them, the Valdosta Kid just pulled his iron and killed him."

"What kind of name is that?" Lodero asked again.

"It's the city he's from, back east. He wants to be a known man, so he named himself something folks would talk about," Mullen explained.

"You said he shot Wash three times in the chest," Lodero said. "Do you know how many shots he fired?"

Jake Mullen closed his eyes and tried to focus on the scene. He tried to count the shots. It was hard, because the shots from these fast gunslingers often ran together and two shots could sound almost like one.

"I know he missed with his first shot," Mullen said. "I remember he throwed his gun and fired, and the shot hit the store behind where Wash was standing. In just that instant, I thought Valdosta was just trying to scare Wash, or provoke him. I thought that because I seen that first shot miss. He may have even got off another shot that missed, but definitely the one."

"You rode with these men for a while," Lodero said.

"Don't put that on me," Jake Mullen said. "I hired on with Nick Noble to rustle cattle. I figured if it came to shooting, I'd do that, too. But I didn't know Nick would hire men like these. And like I told you, everything they said was 'provoke' Wash Scotland. And I knew Wash wouldn't throw his gun. So I thought nothing else would come of it. If I'd thought for a second that they would gun down Wash Scotland the way they did, I would have warned Wash and gotten him out of there. Or I'd have backshot those sons of bitches."

Lodero figured Massey was dangerous. A man in his forties would be considered an old gunslinger, and the only gunslingers who got to be old were the ones who were very good. Massey might have to go first.

The Valdosta Kid was dangerous because he was looking to run up tallies. The boy wanted to be known, and the way to do it was to shoot more men and add more names to his list. But his first shot on Wash missed.

Danny Walker might be a bigger threat. A quiet man who kept his gun in his hand could be a dangerous man.

"If you was me, who would you throw on first?" Lodero asked.

"Walker," Mullen said with no hesitation. "He was born with that iron in his hand. Massey can hit a buffalo from distance with that Sharp's rifle, but he ain't no gunslinger. He's a killer, but not a fighter, anyhow. And second would have to be Valdosta. He's a braggart, but that don't mean he can't throw and shoot. And I seen for myself that he'll kill a man. If it's me, I'm shooting Massey last."

Lodero rubbed his thigh. It was stiff having been in the saddle all day.

"What about Nick Noble?" Lodero asked.

"He comes after Massey," Mullen said. "Nick ain't no gunslinger. My guess is that he'll be out the back door and running before Massey hits the ground."

"Nick shot me," Lodero said.

"Did he get you that day at the creek?" Mullen asked, surprised. "I knew he took a shot or two, but I didn't know he'd hit you."

"Got me in the leg," Lodero said.

"For him, that was a mighty lucky shot, anyhow," Mullen said. "I suppose it was unlucky for you."

"Depends on how you consider it," Lodero said. "Unlucky that he hit me, but lucky he didn't hit me in the head."

Mullen laughed. "I reckon so."

They kept on in silence for a bit, keeping their horses at an easy pace. "Anyhow, you ain't going to be alone. I'm backing your hand, whatever it is."

"He was already not alone," Juan Carlos Baca spoke up from behind the two younger men.

Mulled turned in his saddle and looked back at Juan Carlos. "See there, they's three of us already. I'd all but forgotten about you old man. The odds are evening."

Juan Carlos took offense. "We will see what the odds are when this thing ees done."

Mullen grinned at Lodero. "I reckon he don't trust

me. Can't say that I blame him. But I'm shootin' straight. I'll do for you what I should have done for Wash."

"How much farther?" Juan Carlos asked. The sun was getting low on the distant horizon and the cicadas in the mesquite were beginning their nightly chorale. Soon it would be too dark to see much beyond the road.

"These gunslingers, they've been staying in town at the hotel, but they's a spot down here on the river where the big slabs of rock form a little cave, if you want to call it that. Nick Noble knows the spot. When we've come and run off some of Miss Noble's stock in the past, we camped out here. It's far from the road and far from anything else that would lead men to it. The posse wouldn't never find it, and Nick knows that. They'll be worried now, at least Nick will be, anyhow, on account of this whole thing going sideways with Wash. I don't know how them hired guns will take it, but Nick doesn't like for his plans to go astray. I know the trail to the hideout, and I can follow it in the dark. I also know how we can get up in there and take a look without them seeing us. It'll be best at dark, anyhow. I figure once we've seen how things are, we can get them in the morning at first light."

Juan Carlos urged his horse forward so that he was up even now with Mullen. In the dimming light he nodded down to the shotgun to draw Mullen's attention to it. "If dis goes bad, my scattergun is pointed at you. I'll make sure you don't live through dis."

"I don't blame you none," Mullen said. "But if you want to do your part to keep the odds close to even, you'd be wise to put that scatter gun on one of them others."

15

Armed with rifles and pistols, and Juan Carlos carrying his two-barreled shotgun, the three riders staked their horses in a patch of grass near the bank of the river.

"We're still about a mile away," Mullen said, keeping his voice low. "But we can follow the river to them."

Though there had been some spring rains, the river was still shallow and did not entirely fill its banks. If they stayed up near the bank, the ground was hard and they did not sink in. The men walked silently for some distance with Mullen in the lead. Every ruffle of leather against pant leg or clank as a rifle inadvertently came against a revolver grip, or snap of a twig underfoot seemed to thunder like canon fire in the quiet of the night. An owl or a distant coyote were the only other noisemakers occupying the mesquite. The night was too dark, still, for the men to see much of anything. There was no moonlight to speak of, and they found their way by avoiding the darkest shadows that might be fallen limbs from cottonwoods or mesquite branches or even holes that might trip them up. Lodero caught a whiff of the tangy smell of smoke and put a hand on Mullen's shoulder. Mullen stopped and turned back toward Lodero. Even standing arm's length away, Mullen and Lodero could just make out features on each other.

"Smoke," Lodero whispered, and he inhaled audibly through his nose.

Mullen mimicked him and took a deep breath. "I smell it," he said. "We're getting close."

They continued on a bit farther, Mullen choosing every step with great care. As they went, a gray light began to show in the sky, imperceptible at first, but growing bluer by the moment so that soon they could more easily distinguish the mesquite bushes up on the banks and the broken limbs, and the narrow and shallow stretch of river down beside them. The faint smell of smoke also grew stronger, and soon they heard a horse blow. At the noise, Mullen squatted down low, and Lodero followed his lead. Juan Carlos Baca bent himself a little at the waist, but his girth and his aged knees didn't provide for much squatting.

Mullen edged himself closer to the water and motioned for Lodero to follow. As he did, Lodero could see up ahead a small glow of coals from a fire that had been left to burn overnight. Mullen pointed to the left of the fire. "Do you see the rock hanging over the cave?" he whispered.

Lodero nodded. The cave was simply a large solid slab of rock where the river, over hundreds of years, had washed away the dirt beneath it, forming really more an impression in the bank and a roof overhang than a cave.

"Someone, surely, is on watch," Mullen whispered. "But the rest will be camped inside that cave. Let's go up the bank and circle closer in behind the mesquite."

Again, Lodero only nodded and did not speak. He allows Mullen to go up the bank first, and then followed him.

Juan Carlos Baca came up behind Lodero, but his foot fell into some soft sand and the bank gave way, and Juan Carlos tumbled backwards with an enormous commotion. He dropped the scatter gun, and it banged loudly when it hit a rock.

"Hey!" someone from the camp ahead of them called, and immediately there was the explosion of gunfire as the lookout there sent three wild shots in the general direction of where the noises came from. Neither Mullen, Lodero nor Juan Carlos were struck, but any hope of stealth or secrecy had now gone. The others at the camp now scurried from their bedrolls and there was hollering and chaos as those who were deep asleep woke violently to the alarm of gunshots.

Juan Carlos attempted to scurry up the bank before he was seen, and Lodero offered a hand and pulled the old Ranger up the bank and in behind a mesquite bush.

"The scatter gun," Juan Carlos said, turning back toward the river bank, but Lodero took hold of him and pulled him away.

"Too late for that now," Juan Carlos said.

Now more shots blindly sliced through the mesquite, and Lodero and Juan Carlos bent low to run deeper into the mesquite in search of shelter.

They found Jake Mullen crouched behind a mesquite bush, his rifle up.

"If we can remain unseen, we might yet maintain our advantage," Mullen said.

The two younger hired guns peered down rifle barrels and fired a shot or two apiece into the mesquite. In the first blush they could sight no target among the dark shadows of the mesquite bushes. Mullen and Lodero watched them, and any time the rifle barrels came near to aiming at their unseen targets, the two men would duck low to be sure they were not struck by random shots. The men down by the cave were still little more than silhouettes, though it seemed with each passing minute that they grew clearer in the dawn.

The older man, Massey, worked to saddle the four horses staked nearby, and Lodero saw in the dim light that Nick Noble held Maria Noble at gunpoint. He had her up on her feet, his back to the cave entrance where they had slept, and Nick Noble clutched Maria by the arm, holding her in front of him so that she was like a breastworks, protecting him from any gunshots that might come into the camp. Once those horses were saddled, the four men would be able to mount and make a break with Maria still held as their hostage, and Lodero could make no pursuit.

"Juan Carlos, as fast as you can go back to our hawses," Lodero said. "Stay under the cover of these mesquite bushes until you can safely get back to the river bank, and then go as fast as you can go."

Juan Carlos nodded, but a chill went across his arms and spine, and he shivered at it. As Lodero issued instructions, a gunshot barked out from the campsite and a bullet cut through a mesquite bush not terribly far from them. In this moment, with gunfire ripping through the mesquite, the smell of gun smoke filling their nostrils, the early morning hour -- it all combined to recall to Juan Carlos's mind memories of similar mornings in Mexico with Lodero's own father. In his mannerisms and his tall, strong build, in his dark eyes and sharp nose and chin, Lodero looked so much like his father that for a moment Juan Carlos felt as if he had been transported thirty years into the past.

"I will hurry," Juan Carlos said, ducking through the mesquite even as it tore at his clothes as he passed by a bush and made his run to retrieve the horses.

"We need to try to hold them here if we can," Lodero said.

"We can shoot the hawses," Mullen said.

"Like hell," Lodero said. He'd known too many men in his life who needed shooting, but he'd never known a horse that deserved to be murdered. Gunning down a man was a thing that sometimes had to happen, but shooting a horse was an unthinkable act of barbarity in Lodero's mind.

"Pin them in," Lodero said. "Give them reason to believe they cannot ride out of there."

Lodero and Mullen both understood that they could risk no shot into the camp. Their targets were too crowded near Maria Noble. If a bullet missed its intended victim, it might just as easily hit Maria or strike a rock and ricochet wildly into her. Nick Noble and the three gunmen had selected an excellent position to make a stand. But their ability to escape that place might be limited.

Together, the two men spread out among the mesquite bushes and then fired a wilting volley -- Mullen shooting a few shots to the right of the camp and Lodero shooting a few to the left. These were the first shots they had returned. Nick Noble ducked behind Maria. The one who called himself the Valdosta Kid dropped to his stomach so that he was hidden behind the embankment. The other young gunfighter, Danny Walker, he held his ground and looked for a target to shoot at. Massey dropped a saddle and drew the Sharp's rifle from behind a horse, peering out through the mesquite for a target. Lodero, if he was honest, feared that Sharp's rifle. If Massey had been a skilled buffalo hunter, he could plug a target from a great distance, and that Sharp's could pack a punch that would knock down a buffalo. It would do greater damage to a man.

Mullen changed his position and fired a couple more shots at the perimeter of the camp. Lodero crept nearer, staying low behind the mesquite, hoping to get a clear shot at any of the men. Massey was seeking Mullen, having found roughly the spot where the last shots had originated. His eye looked through the long brass tube mounted on the barrel of the Sharp's.

Looking down the iron sights of his Winchester, Lodero believed he at last had a shot at Massey. Lodero steadied his breathing, and made to pull the trigger, but too late, for the hammer fell on the big Sharp's rifle, and it spit smoke and fire and its lead ball. Massey did not move much with the recoil of the rifle, but the horse that was providing him cover from return fire startled at the loud blast from the rifle, and the horse began to dance. Massey took a step back and swung the rifle up toward the air to clear it away from the horse.

Now Lodero had a clear shot, and he held his breath for just a moment as he dropped the hammer on the Winchester. The bullet caught Massey in the chest and knocked him back. A shout from the camp told Lodero he'd given the man a grievous injury. Now Danny Walker dropped to his knee beside Massey, trying to stop the blood pumping from his chest. Walker was too low behind the embankment for a clear shot. Valdosta was also crouched behind the bank, and Lodero could not get a good look at him. Nick Noble hid behind Maria.

Mullen made no noise, and Lodero did not know if he'd been hit. Seeking better vantage points, they had moved out of sight with each other.

Nick Noble panicked. He pushed Maria toward one of the saddled horses, and at gunpoint forced her into the saddle. Nick took the reins of another saddled horse and swung himself up into the saddle. Valdosta and Danny Walker realized too late what he was doing, and the two horses galloped hard out of the campsite and along the dry bed of the river.

"Hey!" Walker yelled. "Come back here!"

But it was no good. Noble had decided to abandon the hired guns so that he could make his own escape, taking his hostage with him.

There was no reason now not to send shots into the campsite, but Lodero wanted one of those horses if he could get it.

"The posse has you surrounded!" Lodero called to the men in the camp. "You boys toss down your guns and throw your hands in the air and give it up!"

"We ain't been paid to toss down our guns!" the Valdosta Kid hollered back, and he stood up from behind the bank, a revolver in each hand, and he fired several wild shots into the mesquite. Before Lodero could aim and fire, Valdosta dropped back to his knees.

Lodero's only concern now was to pursue Nick and Maria. Every second he wasted with the gunslingers was a second farther Nick got.

Lodero saw Danny Walker crawl away from Massey to where Valdosta was hidden behind the riverbank. He could see that Massey was not moving, and the body in the dirt gave the impression that it Massey's end had come.

Lodero fired another round to dig into the dirt at the edge of the embankment.

"We'll shoot you out of there if we need to," Lodero called. "With the woman gone, there's nothing now to prevent us from unloading on you."

The other two horses remained unsaddled. These men would make no quick break in the way that Nick Noble had done.

Valdosta stood again, both hands full, and he fired off three or four shots from each revolver. The shots were wild, and though they came in Lodero's direction, none came near their target.

But before the Valdosta Kid could duck back down behind the embankment, a rifle shot rang out from somewhere in the mesquite to Lodero's right, and the Valdosta Kid dropped his guns and clutched at the wound that opened up in his stomach.

If Mullen was hit by the shot from Massey's Sharp's rifle, he'd not been wounded so bad that he was out of the fight. Like Lodero, he'd been moving for a better opportunity, and when Valdosta stood, Jake Mullen took his chance.

Valdosta had fallen back into the riverbed, and he was screaming and crying out, but all the noise he made was gibberish.

Danny Walker was now alone, and he had no intention of dying or getting gut shot like his two friends.

Lodero watched him scramble up the far bank, pulling himself over the slab of rock that hung over their campsite.

Walker had now exposed himself, and he made an easy target. Lodero had him sighted with the Winchester. But Lodero did not pull the trigger. He'd never yet shot a man in the back, except the man who'd tried to force himself on his sister. Lodero forgave himself that sin for it had been done to protect his sister, and he was young when he'd done it. Even if it meant allowing Walker to escape and hunting him down later, Lodero was inclined to let him go rather than shoot him in the back.

But Jake Mullen had no such misgivings. A second rifle shot rang out from Lodero's right, and Walker fell off the rock slab and down into the bed of the river.

Lodero and Mullen both stood up from the cover of the mesquite and ran to the river. There they found Valdosta, squirming in the mud and clutching at his wounded stomach, and both Massey and Danny Walker were lying dead. Mullen's shoulder was bleeding. The man who fancied himself the Valdosta Kid was rolling in pain and crying out. Lodero winced as he looked at the boy, and he started toward him to offer some help. But Mullen fired a fatal shot into Valdosta's head, and he did it with less interest or emotion than he would have possessed had he dispatched a horse with a broken leg.

Lodero started to say something, but he stopped himself. He recoiled from the sudden and unnecessary violence. But then he remembered that he'd come here to kill these men for what they'd done to Wash Scotland, and Mullen had come for the same thing.

Mullen saw the internal struggle Lodero had over the execution.

"He's the man that pulled the trigger on Wash," Jake Mullen said. "All I did was give him what he deserved."

Lodero shrugged. "I ain't making a complaint." Lodero looked down at his own white and black checkered shirt, now splattered with Valdosta's blood. He took off his kerchief and attempted to wipe some of it away, but all it did was smear it.

"How bad is it?" Lodero asked, nodding his head at the blood on Mullen's shoulder.

"He winged me is all," Mullen answered. "Ain't hardly a scratch, but it burns like hell."

"Nick rode off with Miss Noble," Mullen said.

"I saw," Lodero said. "I'm going to saddle one of these hawses and give chase."

"No need," Mullen said. "Here comes your black!"

Lodero turned and saw Estrellada Nocturno racing along the riverbed, followed close behind by Mullen's horse. Juan Carlos, mounted on his own horse was in the back, pushing the other two.

Lodero held his hands out wide and stood in front of the horses, and the stallion slowed its gait as it came up to Lodero. He took the bridle and then the reins, and he stepped into the stirrup and swung himself into the saddle.

"I'm right behind you!" Mullen cried, holding out his hands to catch up his own horse as Lodero and the black charged down the riverbed.

The tracks in the river bed were easy to follow, and Lodero rode hard in the hopes of catching the riders who had made those tracks.

16

Lodero knew he had to spare the horse, but he gave the stallion free rein to run as far as he would. There was no way to know where Nick Noble would take Maria or how far Lodero would be forced into chasing after them. Mullen and Juan Carlos were somewhere behind him. Nick Noble and Maria were ahead of him. From the tracks they left, Lodero was able to see when the strides of the horses began to shorten and they slowed their pace. Noble, too, realized that if he was going to get away he would have to do it on a fresh horse. But the stallion was willing to keep after it, and Lodero let him continue his run farther than Noble and Maria had run.

But eventually Lodero came to a place where the bank was freshly disturbed, and he could see that Maria and Nick Noble had driven their horses up the bank and along a trail to the south. The black needed no coaxing and bounded up the bank as if he, too, were following the tracks in the sand. The trail itself was worn and easily followed, but the tracks were not as clearly visible. Lodero had to look for the white flashes of rocks recently scuffed and broken under the shod hooves of the horses. The signs continued, and it was evident that Nick Noble and Maria had continued along the trail to the south.

The stallion was sweating and breathing hard trying to keep up the pace. He'd been ridden all the day before out on the ranch and through the night in pursuit of the hideout. Now in the chase after Nick Noble and Maria, the stallion was growing exhausted. Near a stream, Lodero reined in and dismounted, giving the stallion an opportunity to drink.

"Drink fast old hawse," Lodero said, patting the horse's hind quarter. "It looks like they've rode into town. When this thing is done, I'll take you to the livery and get you brushed up good, some fresh oats, and maybe I'll put a little whiskey in your water. Would you like that hawse? We've had a couple of big days, and I've asked you to do your part. Soon your part will be finished, and then it's just for me to do this one last thing."

Lodero was impatient, but he knew if the horse overheated he would be on foot and might never catch Nick Noble and Maria. Lodero contemplated what Nick Noble's plan might be while he waited for the horse to get its fill. Noble had grabbed Maria in the spur of the moment. The shooting with Wash Scotland had not happened the way the men planned it out. Had they gotten Wash to draw first, their plan might have been successful. They could have shot Wash in self-defense and the law would have let them be over it. Lodero certainly would have come to town looking for justice -- regardless of how the law perceived justice. And, Lodero reasoned, they might well have killed him. That certainly would have opened the door for Nick Noble to scatter Maria's stock. "Critters," Wash called them, and Lodero smiled at the memory of the man. And then he grew enraged at the plotting that led to a good man's murder.

"Damnation, hawse, finish your drink and let's be on with this," Lodero said, and to let the stallion know he meant it, he swung himself into the saddle.

Estrellada Nocturno took the hint and lifted his head from the stream. He blew and stomped his front hooves as if to prove his readiness, and Lodero gave him a squeeze with his knees. The horse bolted forward, ready to run again.

Throughout the chase from the hideout cave, down the riverbed and then along the trail, Lodero kept the tall mountain over the town as a landmark. Since turning onto the trail, the mountain had been roughly ahead of him, and growing larger with each long stride of the horse. It started as nothing more than a thin, blue hump on the distant horizon, but it was taking shape and becoming gray with tinges of brown.

Lodero figured he was now not more than five miles from town. He imagined that perhaps Nick Noble ran to a population in hopes that Lodero would not shoot him in front of witnesses. Or maybe Noble intended to get money and flee. It was possible, too, that he'd gone to the lawyer, Bradford Decker, in the hopes of finding a legal way out of his troubles. This seemed most likely to Lodero. Nick Noble had sought to use the law to steal Maria's ranch, and running to a lawyer with a kidnapped woman as a hostage seemed to fit what Lodero knew of Nick Noble's personality.

Whatever Nick Noble's intentions, it did not matter. Lodero was riding to town to kill him, and there wasn't a man nor a law that could prevent it.

At the top of a rise, the mountain south of town grew larger, clearer. He was close now. He knew, too, that whatever business Nick Noble might have in town would only just now be getting started. Lodero had not lost much ground on Noble and Maria, even though they rode fresher horses, and they would have just now arrived in town. Lodero would be there in less than a half hour if the stallion held his pace.

And now he could see the buildings of town, the wagons and pedestrians in the main street, the activity of ranchers and businessmen and women and children who had no idea that death, borne on a sleek, black stallion, was galloping into their midst.

Bradford Decker's office was near the hotel, and out front of it Lodero recognized the two bays, one with a white face. These were the horses he'd seen Nick Noble and Maria ride away on, the horses he'd been chasing for the last couple of hours.

Lodero drew stares from the folks in town, the people who were going about their business. He was filthy from two days in the saddle. His clothes were torn from brushing up against the mesquite. His shirt was fouled with blood where Mullen had shot Valdosta. No less than the blood on the shirt, the look on his face drew stares. Lodero wore on his furrowed brow a look of rage, and murder danced in his dark eyes.

As he dismounted in the middle of the street and started toward Decker's office, Lodero caught sight of the lawyer sitting at his desk. At the same moment, Decker saw Lodero.

***

As they rode into town, Maria just in front of him,

Nick Noble holstered his revolver.

"Decker's office," Nick said to Maria. "You go off in any other direction or try to get away, I'll gun you down. If you think I won't shoot a woman in the back, then I reckon you don't know me well enough."

But Maria Noble had no doubts about her dead husband's son. She knew he'd make good on his threat, and so she did as she was told. She was still overcome by what she'd witnessed, here on this street, the previous day. First the taunting of the good, kind-hearted Wash Scotland. He'd taken it. They'd said things to him that no man would endure, but Wash Scotland, thinking of his wife and his children, did endure it. He took it and he never even touched the gun on his hip. And when he refused to draw, that cruel young man -- just a kid who had no concept of the value of life or what it meant for a man to be too deep in a grave to raise his children -- that cruel man shot and killed Washington Scotland. Maria was left stunned and horrified, her heart broken for her foreman. And then Nick had jerked her off the ground and pushed her down onto the front of his saddle, the pommel digging painfully into her side as her body bounced against the gait of the horse.

Through the night she was cramped into the back of the washed out cave, though it wasn't really a cave. She did not sleep. Every time she closed her eyes she saw Wash's eyes get wide as the shots hit him.

Nick and these hired guns spent most of the night talking. How could they still work the situation to Nick's advantage? Nick plotted and schemed. The other men did not much care.

"You paid us to do a job, and we're doing it," the oldest of the three men had said. "You want this feller

Lodero dead, we'll kill him. What happens with the ranch after we're done ain't none of our concern."

"If I don't get this ranch after you're done, then you killing him don't help me none," Nick said. "You weren't supposed to gun down the nigger soldier. You were supposed to coerce him into throwing on you and then shoot him. It had to all be done legal."

In these discussions, Maria learned what their plan had been and came to understand that the murder of Wash Scotland had been the scheme fouled up. They thought they could taunt him into pulling his pistol, and when he didn't they murdered him anyway.

Likewise, they had fought over her. The older man of the hired guns -- they called him Massey -- he had berated Nick for grabbing Maria and bringing her to the hideout.

"Posse'll be on us for sure, now," Massey had complained.

But Nick's only thought was how to turn the present situation into his advantage to secure the ranch for himself. In the end, Massey argued that if Nick needed Lodero dead before, he still needed him dead now. And Massey said he and the other two gunslingers would finish out the job they were hired to do, and Nick should talk to his lawyer if he wanted to get the ranch legal.

Maria did not cling to hope for her own salvation. She believed it would come and that she would be released. But she was too sorrowful to even think of her own safety. She did not know if she would find an opportunity to escape or if somehow Lodero would find her. She believed that he was capable, that he might find her, and if he did that he would save her. But she was also confident that when her chance came, she would recognize and take that chance. And through her confidence, she put aside her own fear, and instead thought only of Wash and his poor wife and children. She determined then, during the night, that when she was free from this she would hire Wash's wife, Junie, to cook and clean. She and the children could continue on in the foreman's house. She would see to their future.

Maria watched through the night as Nick paced back and forth in front of the campfire. He was panicked and angry and scared, and if he sought counsel among the hired guns, they were indifferent. Nick assured them that the hideout would not be found. They planned to ride out to the Noble Ranch at sunup and find a spot where Massey could shoot Lodero from distance with his buffalo rifle. But their plans were interrupted when the gunfire started.

Maria thought it must be the posse that had tracked them down. It seemed there were many men hidden in the mesquite, surrounding the campsite.

While the hired guns were distracted, Nick Noble put his revolver under her chin. He was standing behind her, using her as a shield against the posse's gunfire.

"We're getting out of here as soon as Massey saddles that second horse," Noble whispered into her ear. "If you try anything, I will shoot you dead. When I tell you to go, you run for that front horse, get in the saddle and ride east in the riverbed. I'll be right behind you. And don't forget that I'll shoot you dead if I have to."

And that was how it happened. Maria fled, but was still a hostage.

As they rode into town, Maria hoped against hope that Lodero would be standing on the street, that her salvation would come with a bullet from his six-shooter. She detested Nick Noble and wondered how he could be the son of the man she'd married. Whatever else Nicholas Noble might have been, he was a kind man. He was shrewd in business and had made enemies, to be sure, but he had always treated her decent, and he was good to the men who worked for him. But his youngest son was an apple fallen too far from the tree.

He pushed her through the door of Decker's office.

Decker had seen them coming from the window and he was already on his feet.

"Look here, now, Nick, you can't bring her in here like this," Decker said. "Folks saw you take her after that Negro what works for her was killed. That posse is looking for her, looking for you, and looking for them other three men."

Nick drew the Colt from his holster. He did not aim it or threaten either Maria or Decker with it, but they were both aware that he had the gun in his hand. The Colt added to the tension in the room, but it was plenty tense without the gun.

"Is the posse in your office?" Nick demanded angrily.

"Obviously not," Decker said.

"Then I guess I'm safe here for now."

Nick took Maria by the arm and forced her into a chair. He sat in another chair across the desk from Decker, who also took his seat.

"What am I going to do?" Nick asked. "How can I turn all of this in my favor?"

Decker raised his palms to the ceiling. "I don't

know," he said. "Where is Massey and those other two?"

"The posse is on them," Nick said. "If they're not dead already, they soon will be."

Brad Decker wasn't much of a gambler, but he knew a bad hand when he saw it. But he wondered if Nick Noble's bad hand might be a stroke of luck for him. Decker leaned back in his chair and eyed Maria Noble. Her face was a marble statue of anger. But Decker's mind began to concoct scenarios that might put him in a good light.

"Short of her testifying that she went with you willingly and then her willingly signing over a deed, I don't know how you get that ranch now," Decker said. "The whole town knows you snatched her up and abducted her yesterday. The sheriff is looking for you for that, and for your role in the murder of that Negro. Everyone knows you hired those gunmen in a scheme to get your daddy's ranch, even if they don't know exactly what that scheme was. At this point, Nick, I would tell you that your best move is to get out of town. Maybe even get out of Texas."

"You're as deep in this as I am," Nick sneered.

"But I'm not," Decker said. "All I've ever done is counsel you on the legalities."

"Running off them cattle so she couldn't make her mortgage was your idea," Nick shot back.

Decker stayed calm, even as Nick's temper flared.

"Nick, you're remembering it wrong. We talked about ways that the ranch might become available, but I certainly never suggested that was something you should attempt."

Decker looked at Maria. She remained

disinterested, but he knew she heard. His profession of innocence was solely for her benefit. Decked calculated that Nick Noble would be stretching a rope soon enough, and Decker didn't want to be on the gallows beside him.

"Look, Nick, let me give you some sound advice, here. Leave Miss Noble in my custody. Go out there and get on that horse, and ride like hell away from here. Get yourself back to San Antone, and from there leave Texas. Go somewhere that you don't have to worry about the sheriff's warrant or the Texas Rangers. Forget that ranch and forget Miss Noble."

Now something out the window caught Decker's attention. Neither Nick nor Maria, sitting in front of Decker's desk, could see what he was looking at. But Decker stood up, still looking out the window, and opened a drawer in his desk. He put his hand inside the drawer and wrapped his fingers around the grip of pistol.

"It may be that you're too late in running, Nick," Decker said, watching the man who'd just ridden up on the black stallion lash the horse to the post outside. "I believe Miss Noble's man is looking for you."

***

As Lodero wrapped the stallion's lead around the post a couple of times and tied it off, he kept his eye on the lawyer on the other side of the glass window. The man stood up and slid open a desk drawer, and Lodero figured he was going for a gun.

But just then a commotion at the opposite end of town caught Lodero's attention, and he glanced down the road to see what was happening. The twenty or so riders coming down the street must be the posse -- coming into town from the opposite direction of where Lodero and

PEECHER

Mullen had found Maria. As Mullen predicted, they'd never been close to catching Nick Noble and his hired guns or to rescuing Maria. But they were here now, and Lodero intended to use them.

He took several steps backwards, back into the street where he'd be well seen by everyone.

"Lawyer!" Lodero yelled at the window. "I'm here for Maria Noble. Send her out unharmed, or I'm coming in to get her."

The man with the tin star on his chest leading the posse urged his horse forward, riding toward Lodero and looking with curiosity toward Decker's office.

Lodero kept his eye on the lawyer in the window. Decker raised his hands to show they were empty and took a step backwards, away from the window and toward the back wall. Just then, though, Decker dropped to the ground, out of view. For an instant, Lodero was confused, but then Nick Noble stepped into view in the window. Lodero's focus was drawn to the small black hole, aiming right at him from the end of the revolver in Noble's hand.

The events did not form in Lodero's mind as thoughts, so much, as just an instant awareness of what was happening. The sparks and flame burst from the gun as Nick Noble fanned the hammer. One lead bullet, two, three, smashed through the large plate glass window, shattering glass, and Lodero saw the breaking apart of the white, stenciled words "Bradford Decker Attorney At Law." Did he see the bullets penetrate the glass? It seemed that he did. The sudden impact of the first bullet was painful and spun Lodero halfway around. The surprise of the thing is what dropped him to his knee there in the street. But when he had a moment to collect his thoughts -- just a moment --

158

Lodero realized that the bullet had merely grazed him, cutting him across the side just below his armpit. He was bleeding, and the wound stung like the devil, but it was a small enough injury and he would survive. The first bullet grazed Lodero, but when Nick started to fan the gun, his aim was all off. He fired five bullets, total, fanning the hammer and sending all but the first bullet high of his target.

The shock of it was over, and Lodero's right hand clutched his revolver. From his knee, he drew the Peacemaker, thumbing back the hammer, and bringing it level with his face so that he was looking down his arm and over the barrel at Nick Noble whose hand was perched over the hammer of his own revolver. Lodero's left hand flew up to the revolver, his left hand cradling his right to steady his aim, his left thumb out and ready to cock the hammer for a second shot.

Lodero let loose the first shot and his aim was too good -- rather than striking Nick Noble, the bullet crashed into Noble's six-shooter and rattled the gun out of his hand. If he'd been content with letting Noble live, it would have been a one in a million shot, but Lodero was there for blood. He thumbed back the hammer as his right trigger finger held the trigger all the way down, and the Colt sent another round into the gaping window. But stunned from the impact to his own gun, Noble ducked out of the way even before Lodero fired the second shot.

From inside the office, Maria screamed.

Lodero released the trigger and cocked back the hammer so it was ready to fire, and he dashed across the street, over the boardwalk and leapt through the frame of the missing window. Glass was all over the inside and outside of the office, and Lodero landed awkwardly as his boots slid through the shards. Noble and Maria were gone from the office. Brad Decker poked his head above his desk, and Lodero jutted the gun menacingly at him.

"Don't you follow me, lawyer," Lodero snarled. "If I see your face, I'll reckon you're planning to backshoot me. You follow me, and I will kill you dead."

Decker raised up empty hands. "This ain't my fight!" he swore.

Lodero's eyes dropped to the busted gun on the floor.

"He's got another pistol," Decker said. "He's still armed."

Lodero gave a moment's thought to shooting Decker right there in the office. The lawyer had turned helpful too fast, and Lodero knew the man was already weaseling his way out of any responsibility. But shooting the unarmed and cowering lawyer now would be nothing less than murder, and Lodero knew people on the street were watching.

Outside the office door there was a hallway leading to the back of the building. At the back of the hall was a door standing open to a back alley where the backs of the buildings on Main Street faced the backs of the buildings fronting Second Street.

Lodero ran the length of the hallway and out into the alley, aware that behind him the sheriff and some number of the posse were entering Decker's office through the front door.

As he came out into the alleyway, the sudden noonday sunlight temporarily blinded him, and to his left

Lodero heard a shot that splintered the door frame not far from his head. Lodero ducked and turned toward the gunfire, his eyes adjusting so that he saw Nick Noble, a gun in one hand and Maria's arm in the other, darting between two buildings and running back toward Main Street. Lodero did not hesitate and+ gave chase behind them.

He was more cautious as he came to the edge of the building where he'd seen Noble and Maria disappear, edging around the side in case Nick Noble was there waiting to ambush. But as he came to the space between the two buildings, he saw Noble and Maria running out into Main Street. Again, Lodero dashed after them.

As he neared the road, Lodero could hear the noise from the street. It seemed that everyone in town was drawn by the sound of gunshots out to the road, lining the boardwalks. When Noble dragged Maria into view, there were screams and loud gasps. They were out in the widest part of the street, a big square with the town's market on one side and the courthouse on the other, with a large hotel next to the courthouse. This was the busiest end of town, and the crowd seemed to be everywhere. There were four or five wagons drawn up in the middle of the road here, and other wagons at a standstill in front of the market. Mounted men were nearby, and other men just standing and watching. Brad Decker and the sheriff and the posse were coming down the middle of the road, crowding the thoroughfare itself.

This was the scene that Lodero stepped into as he came out from between the two buildings, but like a giant stage for a traveling show, the road in the center of the square was cleared of all traffic so that it was only Lodero, Nick Noble, and Maria.

As Lodero entered the stage, the crowd fell mostly silent, or at least seemed to.

"Turn loose o' that woman," Lodero called to Nick.

Noble, crowded in on all sides and trapped upon the stage he himself had erected, spun in the center of the street, dragging Maria around so that she stood in front of him like a shield. He brought his gun up to Maria's head, and women in the crowd screamed out and gasped in shocked horror. Men shot each other sometimes, but none of them could imagine a man treating a woman in such a fashion. The men, who likewise could not imagine such a thing, paled at the sight, and several of them dropped hands to their own guns. If Nick Noble were to pull that trigger, the only question would be which man among the town's populace would be the first to deliver a fatal shot.

Noble's face was contorted in desperation and panic. He'd played out his hand, and the jackpot was being swept away from him. The only play he had left was to spoil the game by murdering Maria, and Lodero, if he could.

"I reckon you ain't got nowhere to go," Lodero said. "Throw your iron on the ground and turn loose o' that woman."

Lodero stood like a statue, his Colt extended in front of him, both hands grasping the grip, his eye squinting down the barrel. Could he fire a shot past Maria to hit Noble in one of the exposed parts? Lodero could hit Nick Noble in the head, maybe the shoulder. But he feared the margin for a mistake. Shooting at a live man standing square behind the woman Lodero loved was a lot different than shooting at cans on a fence post.

"You throw your iron on the ground!" Noble shouted back. "If you don't do it, I swear to God I'll kill her."

"You ain't got nowhere to run," Lodero said. "Turn her loose."

"If I ain't got nowhere to run, then she'll die with me," Nick Noble said. "Why does my daddy's whore get to have the ranch?"

At the slur, women in the crowd gasped again.

"Nick, you best turn her loose!" It was the sheriff come up from the crowd on the street, stepping out onto the stage. "This thing ain't going to work out for you now, but you murder her and you'll hang."

"You murder her and you won't live long enough to hang!" someone from the crowd shouted.

Lodero felt the heat of the tension. It was hard to breathe. He wished this crowd would go on home. Maybe, if there weren't women screaming and men shouting out, there could be a resolution to this. But the crowd seemed to heighten the antagonism.

Noble turned his head first left and then right. He was sweating beads, and desperation clung to his features.

Just then Lodero saw from the corner of his eye a mounted rider's shoulders and legs bounce, a movement he'd seen a thousand times and recognized instinctively as a man urging a horse forward. The man was behind Nick Noble, and Nick knew nothing of it. Lodero hesitated, but shifted his eyes off his target to see the man riding out from the crowd, forward from the spectators and onto the stage, and with a sudden chill going up his spine, Lodero realized the mounted man riding toward Nick Noble was Juan Carlos Baca.

The horse stepped out of the crowd and then had a burst of speed, coming on out at the gallop, charging down on Noble, and Juan Carlos drew a long barreled revolver from its holster.

Again a gasp went across the townspeople, all wondering if this was going to be the moment of violence.

The horse cleared the distance in seconds, and as it neared, Nick Noble became aware of the apparition riding down upon him. He spun his head, turning his entire body as he looked back to see Juan Carlos Baca. Reflexively, Noble moved the gun away from Maria's head to fire a shot at Juan Carlos.

But turning toward Juan Carlos, Nick Noble exposed himself in profile, the full length of his body now visible and open as a target for Lodero. And the barrel of his gun was moved harmlessly away from Maria's head.

Lodero's Colt exploded in flame and smoke. The bullet struck Nick Noble under the armpit, shattering the inside of his chest.

At the same moment, as the horse darted past close enough to touch, Juan Carlos Baca's Colt exploded in flame and smoke, the bullet blasting into Noble's neck and lodging into his spine.

Maria fell away from the violent death, and Nick Noble fired off one wild shot in the throes of death.

Lodero ran to Maria's side, sliding into the dirt beside her to be sure she was unhurt.

Juan Carlos reined in his horse and wheeled back to Nick who was slumped on the ground. The old Tejano slid from his saddle and kicked the gun away from the dead man's hand.

Others in the crowd now darted into the stage, the

sheriff and other men who'd been enraged at the treatment of a woman.

"If he ain't dead, get a rope!" someone shouted.

"Get a rope even if he is dead!" someone responded.

"Everyone get back!" the sheriff yelled, pushing away townspeople. Men from the posse tried to help him clear folks away from the body.

Lodero helped Maria to her feet and held her tight against him, whispering to her as she released the fear and the sorrow of the last twenty-four hours in violent sobs.

Juan Carlos Baca was laughing at Lodero's back. "The old Tejano Ranger still has eet!" he proclaimed loudly, and Jake Mullen was there, too, grasping Juan Carlos by the hand and congratulating him.

But the noise and the crowd melted away from Rosita Maria Rios, the Widow Noble. She heard only the steady breathing of the man she loved, felt only his strong arms holding her safely as she wept for the memory of Wash Scotland and the future of his wife and his children.

"Take me home," she whispered into Lodero's chest.

Without letting go of Maria, Lodero turned slightly toward Juan Carlos Baca and Jake Mullen. "I'm taking Maria to the ranch," he said. "If anybody wants me about this, I can be found there."

17

The sheriff made a journey out to the ranch a couple of days after the shooting, but he wasn't interested in questioning Lodero or attempting to lay blame. Instead, he came with hat in hand to issue an apology.

"It's ain't like folks didn't know what was happening," the sheriff admitted. He spoke to Maria and Lodero with his eyes on the ground. "We all knew Nick was trying to get the ranch. Nobody lifted a finger to help you. And folks didn't pitch in last year for the roundup. Didn't help you when you needed it. And I figured so long as everything was within the law it weren't none of my business. But it got out of hand, and when I should have stepped in, I didn't. Nick hired them gunmen, and that should have been when I stood up and stopped it. But when a person lets a thing go on so far, it gets hard to get control of it after a certain point. This thing went on too far, and it got hard for me to get control of it."

After Nick Noble was shot, Jake Mullen took the sheriff out to the hideout. Jake, having been in Noble's employ, told the sheriff all he knew of Nick's schemes to get Maria's ranch, and Mullen confessed his part in them.

"I wouldn't even know what to charge you with if I wanted to arrest you," the sheriff told Lodero. "It's plain that there was a conspiracy, that Nick and them other men was in cahoots to murder you and steal cattle. And I reckon if I did find some charge to bring against you, I couldn't call a jury together around here that would convict. Fact is, after what happened in town, you and that Mexican feller is both kind of heroes, now."

"He's Tejano," Lodero said. "He fought with the Texas Rangers in the war with Mexico."

The sheriff raised his eyebrows. "Well, I don't guess that would lower anyone's opinion of him, neither."

"What about Jake Mullen?" Lodero asked.

The sheriff took a heavy breath. "I suppose that's up to Miss Noble. He confessed to me that he'd made efforts to run off her stock. I could charge him with rustling based on his confession to me. Although, I wouldn't hold him for Wash Scotland's murder. I don't believe he had no part in that."

Maria looked to Lodero. "Mullen came here to get me and helped me against them hired men," Lodero said. "I reckon it would be a poor way to repay him to swear a warrant. I don't think it's too much to say he risked his life trying to get you free."

Maria nodded and said to the sheriff, "I will not want charges filed against Mr. Mullen."

"He's in town now," the sheriff said. "I know you've got the roundup in a week or so, and I know Jake's looking for work. He's a good man. I've knowed him all his life. He just fell in with a bad bunch."

The sheriff looked at Lodero, wondering about the relationship between the widow and this stranger who had killed Nick Noble in the middle of town. He said to Maria, "I don't mean to overstep, but I know if you're looking for a foreman, Jake Mullen would be a good choice." The sheriff nodded slightly at Lodero. "Of course, you may not need a new foreman."

Mullen had brought Blake Alsworth and Sam Lawrence to the ranch to watch the stock, and Maria had already hired them on to stay as ranch hands. It had only been a couple of days, but they both stayed sober and got to work early and there'd been no trouble with them.

"It might be a good idea," Lodero said to Maria. "It's your ranch and your decision, but there's work needs to be done here, before and after the roundup."

Maria gave Lodero a sharp look. They'd not talked about it, but she knew. She finished his thought for him, "And you won't be here to do that work after the roundup?"

"That's right," Lodero said.

Maria's face registered her sadness at the thought that Lodero was leaving. But she knew, too, as a rancher she had to make decisions about the future of the ranch.

"Yes, Sheriff, I'd be grateful if when you get back to town you'd ask Jake Mullen to come out here," Maria said. "Let him know I have a job for him here if he wants it."

Lodero walked the sheriff out of the house.

"You ain't staying?" the sheriff asked.

"I have business to tend to. My intention is to come

back, but I don't know when that will be."

The sheriff gave Lodero a grave look.

"Having seen you shoot, I'd hate to be the man you have business with," he said.

***

Jake Mullen rode out the next day, and Maria hired him as her new foreman. He did not complain that he didn't have his own cabin and had to share space in the bunkhouse. The foreman's house was still occupied by Wash Scotland's wife and children.

A week or so later, as promised, Jimmy Cook and his hands showed up for the roundup, and with Mullen and his two men pitching in, Lodero and Juan Carlos Baca were able to make short work of the trail branding. Jimmy and his men spent one more night on the ranch before driving the herd north to a railhead. In the coming years, the railroad would come through town, as it had in other places, and the cattle drives would no longer be necessary, but now, they were still the most important part of the ranching business.

Lodero had driven horses short distances but had never driven cattle. He'd talked to plenty of cowpunchers who had been on long drives, some all the way to Kansas and other just to railheads in Texas, but the thing he noticed about most of them is that they only ever went on one cattle drive. The experience of their first drive was enough to convince most of them to find other ways to earn a living.

He didn't watch Jimmy Cook leave off with Maria's critters with any remorse or longing. He was glad to see his short-lived career as a cowpuncher disappear with the herd.

He'd accomplished what he said he would accomplish. The Widow Noble's cattle were being driven to market. She was left with a still sizable herd, plenty to grow from with Jake Mullen watching over them.

Juan Carlos Baca sat mounted on a horse beside Lodero, watching the cattle disappear over the hills to the north.

"How long before we leave for El Paso, mi amigo?" Juan Carlos asked.

"Tomorrow," Lodero said. "Ain't no sense in staying any longer."

"Will Miss Maria pay us?" Juan Carlos asked.

"She went yesterday and took a loan from the bank to get her through until the money for the cattle comes back. She said she will pay us out of that."

Juan Carlos turned his mount toward the barn, but Lodero sat a while longer.

He could stay here. The vow he made was to a grave, and the woman in that grave would never know if the vow was kept or not. Lodero's heart told him to stay. His father had gone away and never returned. He sought fortune, and maybe he found it, but he lost whatever years he might have had left with the woman he loved. Lodero ached to think that he might be making the same mistake.

But the vow he made to his mother's grave was also a promise to himself. He had to know, for himself, what happened to his pa.

"We will leave for El Paso tomorrow, old hawse," Lodero said to the stallion. "We will come back here if we can, but we will finish this thing we have started."

He swung the reins and the black galloped back toward the ranch house.

Maria was lounging in a chair on the front porch when Lodero rode up. She was alone at the house.

"I am exhausted," she said. As much as anyone, Maria herself had pitched in for the work of branding the cattle. She was skilled enough to rope a cow and strong enough to wrestle a cow to the ground. Wash Scotland had taught her well.

"You should be," Lodero said. "It's been a rough bit of work, but it's done now and you'll get the money you need to pay off the mortgage and keep the ranch. You've earned it, I'd say."

"I could not have done it if you and Juan Carlos had not come here looking for work when you did. You saved this ranch for me."

Lodero swung out of the saddle and took a seat on the front porch facing Maria.

"You know that I am in love with you, Lodero?" Maria said.

"No more than I love you," Lodero told her.

"Yet you still plan to leave in the morning?"

Lodero did not look at her. He looked at the boards in the porch, at his own boots, but he did not raise his eyes to meet Maria's.

"I have to go," he said. "I have to find out what happened to my father."

They sat together in silence for a long while. A gentle spring breeze came up across the porch. Already the days were getting hot. Lodero chanced a glance up at Maria, and she was looking at him. Her dark eyes were wet with tears.

"I am so sad that Wash isn't here to see the herd make the drive," Maria said, her voice almost like a whisper. "His critters."

She smiled at using Wash's word. "He told me, when you were hurt after they tried to hang you, that I should hold on to you. Wash liked you real well. He said he'd give me away if we got married."

"Married?" Lodero asked.

"Wash had the idea that we should get married." Maria laughed, even as the tears in her eyes began to drop down her cheeks.

"I reckon Wash had a lot of good ideas."

Lodero felt his heart beat heavy in his chest. Passion overcame him, and he stood and reached out his hands to Maria. When she took them, he pulled her from her chair and held her tight against him.

"There is so much loss," Maria said, the tears rolling slowly down her face. "And now I am losing you. I am scared I will never see you again, mi amor, Lodero."

Lodero put a hand into her hair, and he pressed her head against his chest. He wanted to stop her tears, but he could not do the thing that would lift her sadness.

"Every one of us will suffer through loss and sadness in this life," he said. "The toughest man, the bravest woman, we all get broken. You think it didn't break me when my pa left and never came back, or when my mama died never knowing what happened to the man she loved?

"We're all going to lose, because everyone we love is going to die. That old hawse over there? I reckon I love him just about as well as anything in the world. But unless some son of a bitch backshoots me, I'm going to lose that hawse. You think that won't break me?

"And Juan Carlos Baca — he's been like a father to me ever since my own pa went away, and he's been like a best friend, too, all rolled into one. But he's an old man. And I know I'll have to bury him one day.

"But I reckon what's important in life is what we do with those times in between the loss. How much we laugh or drink, sing or love, and how much we do for the folks that matter to us.

"But it matters, too, the sort of people we are. Am I the kind of man who keeps his word? Am I honest and true, and if I make a promise do I keep it?

"I reckon it don't make no sense, on account of her being dead, but I promised my mama I'd go and find what happened to my pa. And I'm bound to do that.

"But I've made a promise to you, too, Rosita Maria Rios, and I'm as bound by that promise as I am to the one that I made to my mama's grave. I'm coming back to you. And I am the kind of man who keeps his word."

Maria shut her eyes and listened to the beating of his heart. She pressed her cheek against him and cradled her head in the curve of arm and shoulder. She felt safe and warm.

"Maybe tonight, before you leave, will you stay with me here in the house? And in the morning, when you and Juan Carlos leave for El Paso, will you make that promise to me again? Will you make your last words to me tomorrow a promise to return so that I have that to hold onto?"

"I reckon I can do that."

the end

Dear Reader,

Thank you so much for starting out on this journey with Lodero and Juan Carlos Baca.

Their quest has just begun, and if Lodero is going to find the answers he seeks, he will have to start in El Paso.

In the 1880s, El Paso was such a violent place that it was known as the Six Shooter Capital. But this is the place where Lodero must go to learn the truth of what happened to his father.

If you've enjoyed "The Noble Widow," I hope you'll continue on this epic journey with Lodero and Juan Carlos as they ride west to "The Six Shooter Capital."

If you enjoy these Westerns, I would encourage you to follow me on Facebook at Robert Peecher Novels where I post about upcoming releases. You can also sign up for my newsletter at roberpeecher.com.

Thanks, and I look forward to seeing you with Lodero and Juan Carlos is The Six Shooter Capital!

- RP

OTHER NOVELS BY ROBERT PEECHER

THE TWO RIVERS STATION WESTERNS: Jack Bell refused to take the oath from the Yankees at Bennett Place. Instead, he stole a Union cavalry horse and started west toward a new life in Texas. There he built a town and raised a family, but he'll have to protect his way of life behind a Henry rifle and a Yankee Badge.

ANIMAS FORKS: Animas Forks, Colorado, is the largest city in America (at 14,000 feet). The town has everything you could want in a Frontier Boomtown: cutthroats, ne'er-do-wells, whores, backshooters, drunks, thieves, and murderers. And there's also some unsavory folks who show up.

JACKSON SPEED: Scoundrels are not born, they are made. The Jackson Speed series follows the life of a true coward making his way through 1800s America – from the Mexican American War through the Civil War and into the Old West. "The history is true and the fiction is fun!"

TRULOCK'S POSSE: When the Garver gang guns down the town marshal, Deputy Jase Trulock must form a posse to chase down the Garvers before they reach the outlaw town of Profanity.

FIND THESE AND OTHER NOVELS BY
ROBERT PEECHER AT AMAZON.COM

Made in United States
Orlando, FL
07 October 2022